Billionaires for the Rose Sisters

A brand-new duet from Rachael Stewart.

Life hasn't been so kind to sisters Jessie and Hannah Rose recently. The loss of their mother and betrayals of the men they once loved have left them both reeling; romance is the last thing on either of their minds. Until billionaire best friends Joel Austin and Brendan Hart upend all their plans...

Read Jessie and Joel's story in
Billionaire's Island Temptation

And look out for Hannah and Brendan's story

Coming soon!

Dear Reader,

Anxiety comes in many shapes and forms. Grief affects us all differently. We grow up with different responsibilities, views of the world and ways of coping with it.

This book was *hard* to write. It wasn't until revisions that I realized why. It wasn't because it was the biggest pile of poop—my fear at the time. It was because I was too close to it.

It struck many a chord, ripping me open, leaving me exposed and vulnerable, just as Jessie and Joel find themselves. There's a lot of me in it—me and a heapload of love, faith and hope for the future.

Maybe spilling my soul into it was a source of therapy, a release, a book that would in turn help me to heal...

I've dedicated this book to my mum and mum-in-law. Both now have passed, but their battles to stay with us for as long as possible led them down very different paths. I love you both, and you readers too for giving me this opportunity to pour myself into my stories. I hope you find comfort in them too.

Rachael x

Billionaire's Island Temptation

Rachael Stewart

HARLEQUIN
Romance

Recycling programs
for this product may
not exist in your area.

ISBN-13: 978-1-335-73705-2

Billionaire's Island Temptation

Copyright © 2023 by Rachael Stewart

For questions and comments about the quality of this book,
please contact us at CustomerService@Harlequin.com.

Harlequin Enterprises ULC
22 Adelaide St. West, 41st Floor
Toronto, Ontario M5H 4E3, Canada
www.Harlequin.com

Printed in U.S.A.

Rachael Stewart adores conjuring up stories, from heartwarmingly romantic to wildly erotic. She's been writing since she could put pen to paper—as the stacks of scrawled-on pages in her loft will attest to. A Welsh lass at heart, she now lives in Yorkshire, with her very own hero and three awesome kids—and if she's not tapping out a story, she's wrapped up in one or enjoying the great outdoors. Reach her on Facebook, Twitter @rach_b52, or at rachaelstewartauthor.com.

Books by Rachael Stewart

Harlequin Romance

Claiming the Ferrington Empire

Secrets Behind the Billionaire's Return
The Billionaire Behind the Headlines

Tempted by the Tycoon's Proposal
Surprise Reunion with His Cinderella
Beauty and the Reclusive Millionaire
My Year with the Billionaire

Harlequin DARE

Unwrapping the Best Man
Our Little Secret
Reawakened

Visit the Author Profile page
at Harlequin.com.

For my mums,
Sandra and Sheena,
Nanny and Granny,
Miss you and love you always,
Rachael xxx

Praise for
Rachael Stewart

"This is a delightful, moving, contemporary romance.... I should warn you that this is the sort of book that once you start you want to keep turning the pages until you've read it. It is an enthralling story to escape into and one that I thoroughly enjoyed reading. I have no hesitation in highly recommending it."

—*Goodreads* on *Tempted by the Tycoon's Proposal*

CHAPTER ONE

JESSIE ROSE CLENCHED her hands in her lap and gritted her teeth.

Below, the ground peeked between the clouds, flashes of vibrant green and sandy white amidst turquoise-blue waters…she should be appreciating it. Should being the operative word.

The plane juddered and she flung her hands out to grip the seat, squeezing her eyes shut. The dual propellors were doing their best to shake her insides out of her body, and she didn't need the added fear that at any moment the rickety and ridiculously small plane would simply fall from the sky.

She was used to the cold sweat, the tightness in her chest…but this was meant to be a holiday, a chance for some R and R, not cause for another panic attack.

Just breathe, Jessie. Breathe and count.

Her counsellor's gentle words were on repeat in her brain.

In…one, two, three, four. Hold…one, two—

The plane swooped and her stomach lurched. She gave the tiniest squeak, her eyes flaring open. Thank heaven there was no audience to witness her losing her cool. Just the pilot, and he was doing everything he could to keep the toy plane in the air. Momentary turbulence, he'd assured her. Nothing to worry about. Nothing at all.

Only…it didn't *feel* like nothing.

And her brain was only too happy playing out every devastating scenario possible. A trick it had perfected ever since Mum's accident a few years ago. An accident that had retriggered her anxiety and swamped her positivity.

She'd masked it well enough—the insomnia, the panic attacks, the fight to function. She'd had to, for Mum. As her carer twenty-four-seven, she'd quit her job, moved back home, quit her life according to Adam… *Adam.*

She shook her head, unwilling to think about him and his sudden departure from her life. Good riddance, her big sister Hannah had said, but Jessie wasn't so sure…not now Mum was gone and she was alone. No purpose, lost and unsure.

Unlike Hannah, who had a handle on everything…

How could her sister begin to understand how it felt when they lived in different worlds? Hannah's was all champagne and caviar, swanky and successful, living it up in London in her flash city pad, with her even flashier husband.

And hers—

The plane dipped again and she bit her cheek,

swallowing the curse that wanted to erupt and shame over her inner whinge.

Her sister had worked hard to get where she was, and it wasn't Hannah's fault that Jessie hadn't been able to find a career she loved. It wasn't Hannah's fault she'd chosen the wrong man to fall in love with. It wasn't Hannah's fault that she'd given up her life in London to return home to their small village and care for Mum.

And though Hannah hadn't come home as often as Jessie would have liked, she got that her sister had her own stuff going on. She also suspected this trip was her big sister's attempt at making up for her lack of presence.

Yes, she'd wanted to coax Jessie back into the land of the living, but there was more to it than that. She'd caught the hint of guilt as she'd sold it to her: *'It'll do you good to get away, get some sun, be looked after...time to reflect, re-energise and be reborn.'*

A smile teased at her lips—reborn? Had Hannah really said that? The phrase was so...hippyish. For Hannah at any rate. Not for their mother, who even on her deathbed had taken Jessie's hand, squeezed it and said, *'Life is the adventure you make it, Jessie—live it, love it, no regrets.'*

Well, she was doing that, or trying to...with her sister's helping hand.

When Hannah had offered her this escape, she'd said no. The idea of staying in a holiday home belonging to a partner in Hannah's law firm, a man she'd only met a handful of times, felt wrong. Especially when she wasn't expected to pay a penny...not that she could afford it anyway. Even her inheritance was a drop in the ocean compared to the level of wealth she was walk-ing—*flying*—into: Mustique Island, exclusive re-treat for the rich and famous, and as far removed from her world as one could get.

But maybe Hannah was right, maybe this break was what she needed. Meds certainly hadn't been the answer. Counselling had helped...kind of. Though nothing could fill the hole her mother had left behind six months ago.

Her phone buzzed inside her bag and she un-clenched her fingers to pull it out. A message from Hannah glared up at her, her sister's timing as im-peccable as ever:

Don't forget to let me know when you get there, Jess x

She shook her head and typed:

If I don't die on the plane first x

Jess! x

JOKE! x

She could sense her sister rolling her eyes, genuine despair in their clear blue depths, and her heart softened with her posture.

Sorry. I will. Just facing some turbulence xx

Since when have you feared some turbulence? x

Since life had got real... She bit her lip, her thumb hovering over the 'Send' button. No, she couldn't say that. It wasn't fair. Not on her sister, or her attempt to treat this holiday as a fresh start. She erased it and went with:

Landing soon. Promise to message so stop worrying. Shouldn't you be concentrating on your next big win? Those cases don't win themselves... x

Right now, you're my priority, not work. Take care, little sis. I love you x

She stared at the message, tears choking up her throat as her chest contracted. Nothing to do with her anxiety now and everything to do with family. What family she had left.

Three simple words, thrown around carelessly by some, but never Hannah. She wasn't one for sentiment. Even after Mum had passed, there'd been an awkwardness, a hesitancy...

Either the panic attack her sister had witnessed

Jessie suffer a few weeks ago had totally freaked her out, or something else was going on with Hannah, and Jessie wasn't sure which scenario she'd prefer.

Whatever the case, she needed to pull herself together.

A, to prove to her sister she was mentally sound and capable of running her own life without her big sister's interference.

And B, to be there for Hannah should she need her to be. Not that she could believe it. Her sister was the strong one. Fierce, independent, career driven…

She raised the phone and typed:

Take care of yourself and less of the little. Love you too xx

She slipped her phone back into her bag and resumed her clenched position…

'Dream vacation and new me,' she muttered between her teeth, 'here I come.'

Joel Austin eyed the surf and toyed with catching a few more waves before the weather truly turned.

It was getting choppy, the waves irregular and unpredictable. But heading back in meant his time was up and he'd rather be wiped out than face a return to reality.

'Mr Austin!'

His head snapped around, his eyes scanning the shore for the person willing to break his peace.

Ah, Anton.

Even from this distance, the man looked harried, and he let out a sigh. Reality beckoned, his life not so much.

'Hey, Anton!' Joel gave him a wave as his board bobbed beneath him, its undulation building with the increasing swells. 'You going to join me?'

Of course Anton wasn't, but Joel couldn't resist the tease, especially when the man's presence could only mean one thing—his best mate, Brendan, was after him.

'Sorry, sir, you're wanted!'

For all the wrong reasons...

Anton waved his mobile in the air to add to his point and Joel sighed. Definitely Brendan.

'I'll be right in.'

Giving the surf one last longing look, he caught the next wave back to shore. He'd been out for hours already. He might be an arse, on occasion, but, when his best friend had given him the use of his holiday home and all the luxury that came with it, the least he could do was keep his staff sweet.

He hopped off the board, yanked it against his chest and stepped through the foam, his trusty smile pasted in place. This wasn't Anton's fault. It wasn't Brendan's. It was his own. And no amount of surfing the waves or living his life to the max would fix it...try though he might.

'What's up?' He combed his hand through his hair as he paused before his friend's butler and feigned ignorance. He knew exactly what was wrong.

'Mr Hart's been trying to call you, he knows the storm is incoming and wants to make sure your plans are still in place.'

'You mean my exit plans?' He gave him a lop-sided grin. 'Tired of me already, Anton?'

The man's deep brown skin flushed deeper. 'Not at all, sir. Only we have our new guest arriving and want—'

'Hey, chill, Anton. I'm only joshing with you.'

'Joshing, sir?'

'Winding you up.' He dropped the grin and dipped to grab his towel and phone from the sand. 'It's all good, my flight is due to leave this afternoon and I've not heard otherwise.'

Not that Joel would mind getting stranded here, but Anton clearly would as the man's worried gaze drifted to the horizon and the obvious storm brewing.

'Relax, man, it's all good.' He started off in the direction of the villa. 'So, who's the guest that's kicking me out of paradise?'

Falling into step beside him, Anton flicked him a look. Likely assessing whether he was genuinely disgruntled or continuing with the wind-up, and Joel swiftly reinstated the grin.

The gesture was foolproof. No one questioned

it. They saw nothing beyond the foppish blond hair, bright white smile, and crystal blue gaze… not hiding anything. Anything worth analysing at any rate.

'She is a friend of a friend, I believe.'

'A *she*?' Joel cocked a brow. 'Is there a man-she too?'

'A man-she?' Anton was back to frowning.

'A man to accompany the said she?'

Anton shook his head, choking on what Joel would like to think was a laugh but was more likely to be disdain. 'No. I believe she is travelling alone.'

Interesting.

Maybe a quick call to Brendan wouldn't go amiss after all.

Maybe this short adventure could turn into something a little more adventurous.

'You go on ahead, Anton. I'll pack this board away and give Brendan a call.'

'Very well, Mr Austin. Can I—?'

'Please, please, please, drop the mister, and the sir—it's Joel. Just Joel, okay? We've been over this a thousand times.'

'It's not very usual…'

'And I'm not your usual kind of guest, so humour me.'

'Very well. Can I bring you anything… Joel?'

'I'm good. Are my bags packed?' Another question he already knew the answer to… Brendan's staff were ever efficient.

'Of course, aside from the clothes you asked June to keep out for your journey.'

'Perfect! Then I need nothing more. Thank you.'

He waited for Anton to leave before dialling Brendan's number and his friend picked up in two rings. One day he might even hit three. 'You need to get a life, my friend.'

'And you need to find yours again, my friend.'

He laughed at Brendan's swift retort, masking the painful pang of such a direct hit. He wasn't ready to make any such move. Hell, maybe he never would be.

'You're in no place to judge me when you live for your work.'

'It wasn't so long ago you were the same.'

'And look where that got me.' All humour stripped from his voice, Joel felt the chill seep into his bones and he forced a breath, forced his body to relax as he sensed the tension on the other end of the line. The tension, the sympathy, the blasted pity, and the words that were about to spill from his friend's lips if he didn't get there first.

'Joel, I'm—'

'So tell me, who's the lucky lady you have ar-riving?'

There was a momentary silence, punctuated by a heavy sigh as Brendan battled the need to say what he wanted or permit his change in topic. But tough. Some things were better left unsaid.

'How do you know it's a lady?'

His shoulders eased with his friend's capitulation.

'Anton may have mentioned it…'

Brendan muttered an expletive that had Joel choking out a laugh. 'Did you just swear at me?'

'No.'

'You did.'

'I did.'

'Why in the hell would you…?'

'She's Hannah's little sister,' he said over him.

'As in Hannah, super-sexy-business-partner-in-your-law-firm Hannah?'

'I really wish you wouldn't talk about her like that.'

'And I really wish you'd made your move on her before that jerk of a husband got his sweaty mitts on her, but hey, we can't all get what we want.'

'Jesus, Joel.'

'What? Leon is a jerk. God knows what you ever saw in him. He was clearly only ever sponging off you and your connections and—'

'And right now he's the last man on earth I want to be discussing, so quit deflecting and tell me you're packed and good to go?'

Joel laughed, his eyes returning to the horizon and the delightful storm brewing.

'Are you that eager to see me gone?'

'It's not that. You know you're welcome to use the place as much as you like, but…'

'But you don't want me here when she arrives?'

A delay, then. 'Not particularly.'

He'd be offended if not for the fact he deserved it. In the last year, he'd built up quite the reputation…even if most of it was the press and their hyped-up nonsense. Not that he'd bothered setting anyone straight.

'Fair enough.'

'Look, I'm sorry, Joel, you know I love you but she's Hannah's sister. I can't risk you upsetting her and you've zero restraint when it comes to the opposite sex.'

'I'll have you know, I've plenty, as proven by your great-aunt when she made a pass at me that summer.'

Brendan managed a chuckle. 'Aah, good old Aunt Mags, I miss her.'

Joel gave a mock shudder. 'I don't.'

'But I'm serious—'

'Look, don't worry, bud, I read you loud and clear.'

'Thank you.'

'Thank you for letting me stay here.'

'You've had a good time?'

'The best. This place never lets me down.'

'The place or the guests across the way?'

Joel laughed with his friend. 'You know me, I'm nothing if not social with the neighbours…'

'If only you could be as social with your family.'

Joel pretended he hadn't heard him. 'So, if you

want to change your mind, I'd be happy to stick around and show Hannah's little sister the sights.'

'Don't you have a meeting in Tokyo?'

'Do I?'

'Simon called…'

And just like that they were back to his family. 'Did he, now…?'

'Don't say it like that.'

'How else can—?' A gust of wind cut off his speech and he turned his back to it, tried again. 'How else can I say it when my little brother is keeping tabs on me?'

'He's just concerned, we all—'

'And I'm thirty-five, old enough to go through life without having my hand held. Now, do you want me off this island or not?'

'Joel, that's not how it—'

'It absolutely is how it is,' he interjected, turning as a flurry of activity along the coastline caught his attention. Staff appearing from the flora, collecting anything that wasn't tied down, shutters being drawn on beach huts… Brendan's own being tended to by Paolo, the driver-cum-groundskeeper. 'Look, I need to go. The storm's going to hit soon, and it looks like your staff could use a hand before I leave.'

'They're plenty capable of looking after the place themselves—it's what they're paid for.'

'While I sit back and observe?'

'*No.* You have a plane to catch…*before* the storm hits.'

'Yeah, yeah, keep your knickers on, bro.'

Joel cut the call. He'd feel guilty if he wasn't so irritated by his brother's interfering and his friend's dogged concern.

He was doing just fine.

As for Hannah's little sister…

The sound of a light aircraft approaching drew his eyes to the sky…well, well, well, if it wasn't the woman in question. A little greeting wouldn't hurt. Contrary to popular opinion, he was quite capable of acting the gentleman when required. Especially when presented with a woman as off-limits as she certainly was.

And that suited his bachelor lifestyle just fine.

He had no interest whatsoever in getting caught up where he didn't belong.

No interest at all.

A bit of light flirting, on the other hand…now, where was the harm in that?

CHAPTER TWO

JESSIE BLINKED AND blinked again, rapid fire.

She could blame her sudden tic on the blinding sunlight. Her gawping mouth on the incredible, out-of-this-world villa nestled amongst the luscious vegetation stretched out before her. But the true reason…

Six-foot-plus hunk of male perfection stalked through the garden, several wooden boards hooked over one shoulder, sun-kissed waves to his shoulders and a grin to die for.

Or was that his body…?

Half-naked, sweat glistening in the midday rays, exertion showing in every straining and exposed muscle…

He was the entire package and her fired-up, well-neglected body knew it.

She shouldn't be surprised by such a sight either—this *was* Mustique Island. Looking good was probably part of the job description.

She had the impulse to lick her lips…would have done if not for Anton, butler to the incredible holiday home, waiting for her at the edge of the path.

Dressed in beige trousers and white short-sleeved shirt, he was ultra-smart. His smile, respectful and welcoming. His warm brown eyes showed no sign of judging her state of dress, which she had to admit had seen better days. Her tan linen trousers were rumpled through travel, her loose cream camisole was half untucked, and her auburn hair was in wild and frizzy disarray.

Though the man across the way…it was clear the smart dress code of the interior staff didn't extend to him. Was he the handyman…a gardener? She didn't know but she'd likely have more in common with him than the owner of this fine establishment, who must be out of his mind to let her use it for so long.

Staff, accommodation, private transport, no expense spared and costing her nothing.

Faced with the true magnitude of the gift, she had to pinch herself…and not for the first time wonder at Brendan's true intentions where her sister was concerned. Who did stuff like this for someone they didn't know unless it was for someone they'd like to know much better? And yes, she meant it in the biblical sense.

'Come, Miss Rose.' Anton caught her attention, taking her battered suitcase from her grasp, and she almost snatched it back, embarrassed of its state. But all he did was smile kindly—there was no cocked brow, no disapproving tilt to his nose. 'A refreshment perhaps and then I will give you a tour. Mr Hart tells me you've travelled all the way from England.'

She smiled, nodded, but the grimy layer of travel seemed to thicken under his gaze, and the idea of walking through this enormous and sure to be pristine home before freshening up didn't appeal.

'That would be amazing, but I'd love a shower first, if that's okay?'

'Of course it is. Whatever you wish, we're here to provide.'

'That sounds heavenly.'

'I only wish I could save you from the weather.'

Her step faltered. 'So it's true, there's a—a *hurricane* coming? I heard the pilot saying something on his radio but I'd kind of hoped...'

Kind of prayed that she'd misheard him. Hurricanes and her mind were not a good mix.

'Don't worry, we won't get hit directly but the weather's going to get a little rough. I hope it wasn't too bumpy on the flight.'

'It was...fine.' *Liar.*

'We rarely get affected this time of year, but this one's coming a little close.'

She swallowed. 'Just my luck.'

He turned to eye her, taking in her forced smile, the widening of her eyes. 'Don't worry, Miss Rose, you'll be perfectly safe.'

She nodded, wishing she could believe it.

'Anton, shall I leave these here?' The half-naked male spoke behind them, his closing proximity catching at her measured breath and cutting it short. He even *sounded* hot, if that was even possible. English too. And, judging by the way Anton leapt, he'd been too focused on Jessie's arrival to notice him until now.

The stranger shrugged his heavily laden shoulder, rippling all those glorious, tanned muscles. 'Paolo says you'll be wanting these boards to secure the front?'

There was a slight roll to his 'r's, a husky, rich quality to his tone…the perfect voice for the perfect body.

His eyes flitted to her, their depths so blue they reminded her of the sea behind them—crystal clear and full of shimmer. The teeniest shiver ran through her middle and she felt her cheeks warm. She looked away, tried to steady her pulse, so preoccupied with her own reaction that it took her a second to realise that Anton had yet to answer.

The man still looked a little stunned too.

Hmm, maybe half-naked guy wasn't supposed to be missing half his uniform.

Anton cleared his throat. 'You really shouldn't be—'

'I insisted, Anton, it's all good.' The man's grin lifted to one side before he turned his full attention back on Jessie and she had the awful feeling her knees were about to give way.

He dumped the wood and closed the distance between them, offering out his hand. 'Joel, at your service.'

She flicked a look at Anton, who was watching

the exchange with a crease between his brows and an element of wariness, or was that disapproval? Was she about to get this Joel *fired*? He was just being nice, surely?

Or maybe it was her own edgy reaction that had him fretting so…?

She launched forward, took Joel's hand in hers for a thorough shake, opened her mouth to speak, but the heat that radiated from his touch had her vocal cords liquefying along with her limbs. His eyes burned into hers, her body sizzled, and she grinned so wide she must have looked like a clown mid-act but all he did was return it.

'And you are?'

'Jessie!' She scraped her free hand through her hair, trying to get it out of her face as the budding wind insisted on doing the opposite. 'Jessie Rose! I've come to stay!'

'Come to stay, hey?' The shimmer in his eyes multiplied. 'You don't say.'

She gave a nervous laugh, cursing her mouth and her brain, which had taken a sharp exit from her head.

'Well, Jessie Rose who's come to stay, it's a pleasure to meet you.'

The soft murmur to his voice had her giggle extending itself against her will. God, he was good. All charm, and smiles, and sexier than—

A throat was cleared to her left. Anton!

Do you really want to get the man fired for fraternising with the clientele?

She snapped her hand back. 'And you… Joel.'

She wiped her palm against her trouser leg, trying to ease its persistent tingle, and he tracked the move. Oh, God, did he think she was wiping him away?

Her cheeks burned deeper, the words to reassure him on the tip of her tongue, but how could she when the truth was more embarrassing…for her, at any rate? And whatever he thought, he clearly wasn't troubled. His smile was lazy, his gaze too as it drifted past them to the sea beyond.

'I reckon we have a good few hours before it's upon us, Anton. I'll go and see what else I can do before I head out.'

'There really is no need…'

'I know, but it's the least I can do.'

'Don't you have more important things to be getting on with?' Anton's tone and elevated brows suggested there most definitely was, but Joel shrugged.

'Not particularly.'

And off he went, Anton's gaze following him as a sigh passed through his body. What was his problem? Wasn't it *good* that the man was helping?

'Okay, Miss Rose. Let's get you inside.'

She let her gaze linger a moment longer on one very firm behind and gave her own little sigh.

How long had it been since she'd felt a thrill on that level?

Not even Adam had given her such an instant kick. He'd had plenty of that sizzling charm though, charm she ought to be wary of now too, and she welcomed the cool, steadying relief of the air-conditioned villa as they entered.

She breathed a contented sigh…then her eyes clocked her surroundings and became fishbowls.

'Wow!'

Anton smiled. 'You approve?'

'I think I've died and gone to heaven.'

He chuckled. 'It does have a peaceful, Zen-like quality about it.'

A young woman stepped forward, immaculate in a white shirt dress, her blonde hair tied back in a smooth ponytail, her flawless make-up subtle and smile polite. She had a tray in hand with a tall red drink, a fruit kebab resting along its top.

'This is June, one of our housekeepers. June, this is Miss Rose.'

June dipped her head and offered out the drink on her tray. 'Miss Rose, welcome to Villa Amani—can I offer you a rum punch?'

It did look delicious, the condensation on the outside of the glass enough to make Jessie's mouth water.

'Thank you.' She returned her smile, hoping she didn't sound as awkward as she felt, and took the glass, careful to lift the kebab first before tasting it. Delicious! Sweet, cold and with just the right amount of alcohol. She hummed her appreciation. 'That's lovely.'

'I'm glad you like it,' Anton said. 'Now, if you'd like to follow me...'

She did like, very much, her gaze drifting over her surroundings in wide-eyed wonder. She'd expected the visual opulence, of course she had. The outside had been impressive enough, sprawling almost as far as the eye could see, the charred teak and grey stone blending into their surroundings with ease, the enormous glass windows reflecting the sky and flora like picture postcards. But inside...it was *vast*.

The entrance alone could absorb the footprint of her three-bed family cottage.

Dark wooden floors rolled into white walls with colourful wall hangings and exposed beams. Evocative sculptures that could be anything the mind desired, woven furniture with plush cushions that begged to be lain upon, flourishing plants that brought the outdoors in, a colossal skylight swathing it all in glorious sunshine.

'Your quarters are this way. I'll point out rooms on the way and give you a full tour when you're ready...'

She nodded, speechless. Was she *really* staying here? For a whole *month*?

Anton gestured to room after room, each designed with a different activity in mind, from the kitchen, to the reading room, the quiet room, the music room, the full-on cinema with popcorn machine and bar, the gym, the lounge, another lounge… how many people did this house host?

Anton told her it had five bedrooms and an external guest-cum-yoga retreat, but surely that didn't justify the need for *this* many rooms. Money did though.

She didn't bother to hide her awe. Anton would already have her pegged as a fish out of water and, in truth, a house like this deserved to be gawped at.

'And this is your room…'

'Huh?' She almost walked into the back of him, as transfixed as she was by the lattice bronze wall with its gold lining, rippling water, and a feature pond at its base slap bang in the middle of the hallway. Like, where else would you put such a thing…?

Anton grinned and she got the distinct impression he was getting as much delight out of her reaction as she was. Turning, he pushed open the double doors behind him and gestured for her to go ahead.

This time she swore she was going to cry. Covering her gasp with her palm, she stepped into the room.

Ahead the sun shone through the French doors, beyond which a private plunge pool glistened, cool and inviting, while a hammock swung between two palms on one side, and a deep sofa called out to her on the other. The main feature of the room was a huge four-poster bed with hand-carved pine-apple finials, white mosquito nets tied back, crisp white sheets and sumptuous pillows.

Art hung on the walls and plush rugs adorned the wooden floor, all in tranquil shades that brought the colours of the sea and flora indoors. A ceiling fan spun overhead, working with the air-con to create a soothing breeze, and she breathed it all in... it was then she noticed the scent too. A mix of jasmine and ylang-ylang. It had followed her all the way through the villa—was it piped in? Was that what the rich did? Paid for the best air possible...? She wanted to giggle.

'It's beautiful, Anton.'

Beautiful and charming and relaxing and she *really* didn't belong here.

'I am glad you approve.' He gestured to a set of stairs off to the left. 'They will take you up to a secluded outdoor bathroom. You have another bathroom through to the right, a walk-in closet, a wet bar—do let us know if there's anything missing and we'll make sure it's stocked. There's also a phone beside the bed which you can use to reach us any time, day or night.'

'Oh, I'm sure that won't be necessary.' Her voice was a hushed whisper. She was struggling enough to believe this was real, and the idea of ringing for service was nuts.

Anton's smile was warm with understanding.

'It's what we are here for, Miss Rose, and Mr Hart will want to know that we are looking after you properly.'

Her smile came easily in the face of his. 'I know, but right now there's only one thing I'd like…'

He gave a dip of his head. 'That shower?'

'There is that,' she laughed out. 'But no, I was going to ask if you'd call me Jessie?'

His brows twitched and she was sure he muttered, 'Not you as well.'

Whatever that meant…

Perhaps she wasn't so different from other guests after all. She could at least hope.

Blowing out a small breath, he straightened as though remembering himself and gave a brisk nod. 'If that is what you would prefer. Jessie.'

Hearing her name in his heavy Caribbean accent made her both blush and smile wider. 'It is, thank you, Anton.'

'Not a problem.' He placed her suitcase down. 'I'll have June come through and unpack while you shower.'

'That won't be necessary.'

'But I—'

'I really don't have much, so it won't take me long.' Much less than what he and June would be used to for sure, but plenty enough for her.

'Very well. Is there anything else I can fetch you?'

She raised her glass. 'This is all I require…this and my shower.'

And the shower was where she was heading. Then hopefully she'd feel more at ease.

So that wasn't supposed to happen…

Joel turned back to see Jessie disappear inside with a bemused Anton.

Was it the fact she was expressly forbidden or something else that had zipped fire through his veins?

Sure, she was cute, in a fish-out-of-water way. Her auburn hair, devoid of any obvious product, had been a crazy halo tumbling around her shoulders, strands sticking to her face that had borne the sheen of heat and travel.

She wore no make-up if the flush to her skin and freckles across the bridge of her nose were any indication. Her soft auburn lashes framed upturned eyes so vivid and blue, he'd felt himself drowning in them before she could even utter her name.

He'd only ever felt that pull once before, and just like that his blood cooled. He'd been there, done that—fallen in love and lost it all.

And he'd be damned if he'd go there again.

Swallowing the sudden boulder in his chest, he shook off the shudder.

Forbidden. That's what she was and that's what this was—a visceral reaction to what he couldn't have. A pleasing distraction too.

Her innocent charm as she'd smiled back at him, lost her voice, acted out of place…it was bound to draw him in when the women in his world acted as if they owned it.

She was intriguing. Charming. Different.

And very much off-limits.

He had his orders…

And since when do you take orders from any-one?

Ignoring the inner gibe that was bound to land him in more trouble, he went in search of Paolo. He'd call the airport shortly, get the low-down on his flight. He wasn't in any hurry to leave, much to everyone's annoyance but his own.

At least he was making himself useful though. Not that Brendan would be pleased. He'd get it in the ear from his best friend when Anton reported back that he had indeed been chipping in with the staff.

But hell, it wasn't in him to sit around while others worked. He may have bailed on his family's firm to live his life to the max, but he had never, not even in his heyday at the helm of Austin Industries, enjoyed watching others work while he sat idle.

And keeping busy with his hands dulled the never-ending noise in his head and pain in his heart…

CHAPTER THREE

SHOWERED, CHECKED IN with her big sister and her tour with Anton complete, Jessie found her way back to the impressive kitchen with its extensive range of supplies.

Was this truly all for her and the staff?

So far she'd only met five—Anton, June, half-naked, easy-on-the-eye Joel... Then she'd been introduced to the chef, Vittorio, and the senior housekeeper, Margot.

Everyone had been friendly and welcoming, asking for her preferences on food and mealtimes, turn-down services, and so on, and as she'd fumbled for an answer to their litany of questions their curiosity had mounted.

She didn't know whether they were horrified to be looking after someone who so clearly didn't belong, or bemused. Either way they didn't comment. Simply smiled and nodded and took note.

Now that she was hunting through the well-stocked fridge, she realised her non-committal responses had probably driven them crazy...

Spying a jug filled with a delicious-looking juice, she grabbed a glass and poured herself some. She took it to the window that looked out over what must be the kitchen garden—an orchard boasting a variety of fruits and a large veggie patch too. All flourishing and happy in the sun.

'Oh, Miss Rose!'

She jumped and spun, only just saving her juice from a swooshing exodos.

June gawped at her, her arms laden with folded linen, her eyes on the glass in her hand. 'I would have fetched you that…you only have to call.'

Jessie smiled over the grimace that wanted to emerge. 'I really didn't mind…'

June's manicured brows twitched up, her glossy lips shaped in an 'O'.

How awkward…

'I assume it's *okay* that I helped myself?'

'Well, you—'

'Chill out, June.'

Jessie's tripped-out pulse recognised the owner of the voice before he appeared. Freshly showered, judging by the damp hair swept back from his face by a pair of shades and the change of clothing…or should that be addition of clothing? He now wore navy shorts with a white T-shirt that merely hinted at the frame beneath.

It turned out that clothed Joel was just as delicious as half-naked Joel.

Oh, get a grip, Jessie…and quit the gawping!

'Joel!' Beneath her make-up, June's cheeks flushed as she touched a hand to her hair. 'I didn't see you there.'

'As the guest…' his lazy grin passed from June to Jessie '…if she wants to fetch her own drink she can do.'

'Of course, I just—'

'You want to do your job, I know, but you have your hands full and Jessie was more than happy to get it herself.'

She blushed deeper, her eyes drifting to Jessie. 'So long as you didn't mind?'

'Of course not. I'd kind of prefer it.'

June nodded. 'I'll just carry on, then…'

She turned and fled, though Jessie's focus was all on an approaching Joel, her breath hitching the closer he got, and she knew her cheeks were as red as June's.

'Thank you for that,' she hurried to say.

'For what?'

'For covering up for my…misstep.'

'Not at all. You'll have to forgive her—she'll be worrying that her grandmother will have her guts for garters if she thinks she's not taking care of you properly.'

'Her grandmother?'

'Old Margot.'

'Oh, right, I didn't realise.'

'Margot's left her in charge while she and Vittoria make sure the villa is stocked up enough should the storm take a turn for the worse.'

She must have paled because he frowned. 'Hey, don't worry—it'll be fine.'

She nodded swiftly and he gestured to her drink. 'That looks good—mango?'

'Uh-huh.'

'Mind if I...?' He reached forward, his tantalising scent overloading her senses as she offered out her glass.

But he wasn't reaching for hers, he was reaching for the glasses on the shelf behind and she leapt to the side. 'Sorry!'

'No bother.'

He gave her a curious look which she fought to ignore, grateful that June wasn't there to witness her behaviour. Hard-working or not, the flutter to June's lashes and preen to her hair, suggested she had a thing for Joel...or maybe they were dating.

Lucky June...

Though hadn't Jessie been sucked in by a pretty face before, all the charm and charisma, easy smiles and lazy grins...blue eyes that danced too?

A pretty face leaves a nasty taste eventually, her conscience piped up, Adam's smile replacing Joel's in her head and she shook off the sudden shiver.

'Not enjoying it?'

Her eyes shot to his. Why, oh, why did he have to notice her right that second?

'No—I love it.'

He grinned. 'Me too. Old Margot makes it fresh every morning.'

He took several glugs, the sight of his throat

bobbing as he arched his head back too capti-
vating by far. He gave an appreciative sigh that
had a reciprocal one rising up within her and she
clamped her teeth together.

'I'm not quite sure what she does to it, but I've
yet to taste anything so good.'

'I'm guessing the trick is in the freshness,' she
said, sticking to the conversation and not her crazy
fluster. 'The orchard looks like it provides plenty
of fruit. Must be wonderful having it right outside the door.'

She was paying the villa's gardens and indi-
rectly him a compliment. Being as he was, she
assumed, responsible for part of it.

'You're probably right.'

She expected him to move on now he'd sourced
his drink, but he leaned back against the counter,
settling himself in, and she didn't know where to
look. Every time their eyes met she felt her cheeks
blaze, her body feeling inexplicably drawn to his.

*Once bitten, twice shy...it's a saying for a rea-
son, Jessie.*

But it seemed her body wasn't listening, too
hyped-up on pheromones that had been dormant
since her relationship with Adam had fallen apart.

It was a moot point anyway. It wasn't as if Joel
felt the same. She was a guest. He was a member of staff. She was a mess and he was...he was
eyeing her as if the drink wasn't all that he was
enjoying.

'So, what do you make of the place?'

'Hmm?' *Chill, body, chill.*

His grin widened as he gestured around them with his glass. 'The villa?'

'Uh…' Was this normal? The gardener, handyman, whatever, just rocking up, helping himself to the fridge contents and engaging with the guests? No one else had treated her quite so casually…

And are you going to answer him?

'I never knew such perfection existed,' she hurried out, swallowed. 'Or I guess I did—I just never thought I'd experience it for myself.'

'Hopefully that means you'll get more from your stay than most. Have you explored the grounds yet?'

'Anton showed me the pool, the tennis courts, the yoga retreat…'

He nodded. 'All the hot spots. Nothing beats the secret hideaways though.'

He gave a wink that sent the blood rushing to her head again and she covered a cheek with her palm. 'Secret hideaways?'

'Where the view is exceptional and the staff don't venture…'

'And yet you know where they are?'

'Sure do.'

'Care to share?' It came out far more provocatively than she intended, and she wanted to swallow her tongue, but the way his eyes sparked—less tease, more serious, and so damn sexy with it…

'Would you like me to show you?'

She huffed out another laugh, the sound as light as her head suddenly felt. Where had all the oxygen gone? Because she swore she wasn't getting enough.

'Are you offering?'

'Do you always answer a question with another question?'

She smiled, nerves making it a little edgy. 'I think you did that first.'

He gave a hearty laugh and it had the butterflies taking off in her belly. Nerves, excitement, giddiness, the heat of attraction all rolling into one.

'So I did. Come on, I have a little time before I have to leave.'

'What, now?'

'Yes, now—you really should see them before the weather hits.'

She grimaced. The reminder of the storm brewing was an unwelcome intrusion. 'Is it going to be that bad?'

'Hopefully just a couple of days of chaos before returning to sunshine and paradise.'

Her shoulders eased with her breath. 'Thank heaven.'

He cocked his head, took another sip of his juice as he considered her. 'Scared of a bit of rough weather?'

'No.' Even to her own ears she sounded defensive, and she screwed up her nose. 'Okay, a little. Hurricanes aren't exactly a thing in the UK.'

'You'll be fine.' He shrugged. 'I promise. When you've travelled as much as I have, they become something of an occupational hazard.'

'You've travelled a lot?'

'I used to with work, and more recently…well, I choose where I go as much as I can.'

'And that includes choosing places to work that exist on the hurricane belt?'

'Sometimes… I like to live a little dangerously.' And he had the glint in his dancing blue eyes to prove it. Eyes that should make her think of Adam and all the reasons she should be running the other way and not encouraging him. This. Whatever this was.

Never mind the rush of excitement now pumping through her veins as she fired back, 'Rather you than me.'

'And yet you've chosen to holiday here?'

'I didn't quite choose…it's more that I was pushed. Plus, I Googled it and figured sixty-odd years without a serious storm made it pretty safe.'

Clearly not safe enough…

Hurricanes and charming, otherwise known as dangerous, men…what else did the island want to throw at her?

His brows nudged north, his eyes sparking. 'You were *pushed* into coming here on holiday?'

She nipped her lip. 'Sorry, that didn't sound

how I meant it to. I'm not ungrateful. Oh, dear, I really do sound it, don't I?'

'No, I just thought it was an interesting way to put it.'

'It's just been a long time since I've had a holiday on any scale and I'm a little...' she wet her lips '...lost and unsettled.'

Was it her imagination or did she see something akin to understanding in his gaze, a connection born of a similar feeling? Or was he just pitying her for being pathetic? Or, worse, boring? Just as Adam had...

She opened her mouth to explain but he got there first.

'Let's face it, you're thousands of miles from home, in a house staffed with strangers, and the word *hurricane* is being thrown around like it's an everyday thing, so I think you're allowed to feel a little unsettled...even if you are in paradise.'

She warmed with his words and the sincerity laced within them, a reminder that he wasn't Adam and this wasn't anything more than a fleeting and therefore very safe connection. 'Thank you...you've made me feel like I'm not so ridiculous after all.'

He studied her for a quiet moment and then he pushed himself away from the counter. 'Right, come on, I'm taking you on that tour.'

She frowned. 'You're serious?'

'Hundred per cent.'

'You really don't need to babysit me, honest.' Maybe he did deem her pathetic after all… 'I may sound a little neurotic, but I'll be fine.'

'I know you will be, you're in paradise—how can you not be?' He gave her that lazy, lopsided grin as he used the description playfully now. 'But I'd like to leave knowing that you've seen the best this place has to offer.'

'Don't you have other things you need to be getting on with?'

Like working, for one…

'Nah, I've done my bit for the day.'

'So…you're clocking off?'

He frowned, gave an awkward chuckle. 'If you want to call it that.'

He placed his glass on the side and looked as if he was about to say something more, when Anton's approaching voice had his eyes darting in that direction.

'We'll go this way.' He upped his pace, tugging open the door to outside. 'After you…'

She frowned…was he worried about being caught not working?

'Are you sure you don't have something else you need to be doing?' She hurried past him, eyeing him over her shoulder as the heat of the day assaulted her.

'Right now?' He pulled the door to, lowered his shades. 'No way.'

Then he cursed under his breath. 'One second.'

He dived back into the kitchen, and she could just make out some murmurings beyond the door—Anton must have collared him—and then he was back, two bottles of water in hand. 'For the hike…'

'The *hike*?'

'You'll see. It's worth it, I promise.'

She swallowed the battering of nerves. Just how far were they going? And what on earth was she doing? Walking off with some charming stranger in a place she didn't know?

Live a little, Jessie…

It was her mother's voice in her head again… though even for Mum this might be a step too far. It most definitely would be for Hannah. But they'd wanted her to get a life, a new one, a full one…try new things, get out of her comfort zone, enjoy it…

Joel certainly looked as if he was an expert in all the above and he was offering to spend some time with her, and maybe it would rub off a little… maybe she could find some of the old Jessie—pre-Mum's accident and the anxiety and her break-up.

The Jessie that was a little wild and carefree.

And doing it in a place where no one knew who she was—no Mum, no Hannah, no Adam, no judgement—it was as though the cuffs were off and she could do whatever, be whoever, safe in the anonymity of it all.

She smiled, her head suddenly light, her words easy for the first time in a long while. 'I'll hold you to that.'

* * *

Okay, so maybe he should have put her straight the moment she'd made it clear she thought he was a member of staff.

But hell, to be anonymous and treated as an equal by someone so sweet, so normal, so uniquely appealing...

Someone who didn't know his past or care about his future and what he was doing with it...

It felt too good.

And where was the harm?

He'd show her the most amazing spot on the island and then leave as promised. No harm. No foul. No promise broken.

Setting off in the direction of the coast, he chose the uphill path that took them through the palms and gave the most shade.

'It really is beautiful here—' she was fanning her face as she said it '—but I don't know how you work in this heat.'

'You get used to it...'

The heat not the work, so technically he wasn't being deceitful.

'I suppose if I could work in surroundings like this, I'd get used to anything.' She took a deep breath and sighed. 'The air smells amazing too.'

'It comes from all the flowers. The bougain-villea bushes grow wild here and the little white flowers you can see poking through, that's star jasmine. The frangipani trees have quite the scent too…makes me glad I don't suffer with hay fever. I'm guessing you don't either?'

She shook her head, looked to where he pointed, squinting against the sun to take in the trees. 'They're beautiful.'

'And you should have brought your sunglasses.'

'Well, I wasn't expecting an impromptu trip out.'

He took his off and passed them to her. 'Here, you can borrow mine.'

She eyed them with a laugh. 'I can't wear those.'

'Yes, you can.'

'I'll look ridiculous.'

'Are you saying I have bad taste in shades?'

'No…' She pursed her lips, her blue eyes sparkling back at him. 'I'm saying they're too big for me.'

'What if I promise not to laugh?'

She shook her head, caving as she took them and slipped them on. 'Well?'

'Simply stunning.'

Her grin lit up her face, her cheeks nudging into the frames. 'You're laughing inside.'

'I am not.'

'I can tell by your eyes…'

'Is that so?'

'They're laughing, for sure.'

Now he did laugh, realising that if he told her he was being honest, she'd likely run a mile. What was it about this woman?

Sealing his lips on the confession that would

take him one step closer to breaking his promise to behave, he moved on.

'I have to admit,' she said, some quiet steps later, 'I thought the island was called Mystique not Mustique.'

'Mystique is certainly more appealing than the true origin of its name.'

'Really? Why?'

'You don't know where it came from?'

She shook her head, swiping the sweat from her brow with the back of her hand as he offered her one of the water bottles.

'Thank you.'

He waited as she opened it and took a long, satisfying swig. He *tried* not to watch, tried not to react to the sight of her mouth around the opening, the delicate arch to her neck as she tilted her head back...

'So...' she met his gaze as she screwed the lid back on '...you were saying?'

'I was?'

He could just make out the crease forming between her brows, the large lenses of the sunglasses reflecting his own perplexed look back at him.

'You were telling me about the name...?'

'Aah...' *Yes, pay attention to the conversation, not the beauty, Joel!* 'I'm not sure I should say... I don't want to ruin the romance of the island for you.'

'The romance?' She gave him a shy smile, a

fascinating combo of innocence and flirtation, just as she'd projected in the kitchen. 'I'm travelling alone and you're worried about killing off the romance?'

His pulse gave a dangerous kick, his laugh tight. 'Fair point.'

But now all he could think about *was* the romance of it. Of the scent through his nose as he breathed in deeply, the sound of the wildlife and the waterfalls dotted throughout the grounds mixing with the waves rolling on the beach in the distance, and the sight of her, Jessie, flushed cheeks, lips parted in genuine wonder…

Just keep moving, eyes on the track…

'So, the name?'

'The name…' He nodded, grateful for the reminder as he picked his way through the trail. 'How much do you know about the island?'

'Considering that a few hours ago I thought it was called Mystique—not a lot.'

He pressed a straying palm frond out of their path and guided her through, careful to keep his eyes averted. 'It was bought by a wealthy Scottish lord back in the fifties. There were no roads, no jetties, no running water…what it did have, though, was an abundance of mosquitoes.'

'No!' He could feel her astonished expression on him and grinned.

'Yup. Mustique is a corruption of the French

word for mosquito…you're staying on the island of mosquitoes.'

She gave a vocal shudder. '*Ew…*'

'Don't worry, he got rid of his fair share and gave the land the luscious green appeal you see today. He also gifted a large piece of land to Princess Margaret, which was a clever move on his part.'

'Driving the demand of the rich and famous?'

'Precisely. It's now an island owned by its homeowners and ready to be enjoyed by lucky guests like yourself.'

'I do feel— *Oh!*'

She pressed her palm to her chest, her mouth taking on its delectable 'o' shape again as they emerged from the undergrowth onto an outcrop of land shaded by the overhead palms.

From here the clear turquoise waters stretched for miles, the distant islands of St Vincent and the Grenadines punctuating the horizon with sailboats dotted in between. Even the turning of the weather couldn't detract from the awe-inspiring view, and for a moment he took it in with her… his favourite spot on the entire island, happy to be free from reality still.

'I'm surprised the trail isn't more worn with this being at the end of it,' she murmured, lowering herself to perch on the trunk of a wind-bent palm.

'You can only access it from the villa and, as you've witnessed, it's a bit of a trek. But with the constant breeze from the sea and the shade from the palms you can sit here for hours and just look out.' He joined her a safe distance away, his eyes trained on the view. 'If you're quiet enough, you'll have a friend come and join you too.'

She smiled and frowned in one. 'A friend?'

'A tortoise or two, an iguana, a heron, maybe even a hummingbird...'

'No wonder you choose to work in places like this.' Her eyes drifted back to the sea. 'If life had worked out differently, I could have seen myself quite happy doing the same.'

There was something so wistful, so final in her voice that it smothered the momentary pang of guilt that he hadn't set her straight. 'You sound like you think you're past it?'

She laughed, pressing her palms into the trunk as she leaned back and stretched her legs out before her, their freckled lengths tugging at his gaze.

'I *feel* past it.'

He gave a disbelieving laugh. 'You can't be much older than twenty—'

'Twenty-eight.'

Older than he thought. Didn't make her any more attainable though. 'Still, plenty of years left to change the course of your life and do something different if you want to... What is it you do now?'

Her frown made a return. 'Not a lot, it would seem.'

'And what does that mean?' Maybe they had more in common than he'd first thought…

He sensed her gaze sharpen behind the shades, the sudden tension in her limbs, and for a moment he wondered if he'd pushed too hard, but then she shrugged. 'I used to have a job, a plan, I knew what I wanted, or at least I thought I did. I had a career, a fiancé, a life in London…'

'But not any more…?'

He couldn't see her eyes but he didn't need to— he knew their light had dimmed, that he'd ruined the moment with his intrusive questioning. And he should know better than most when to stop pushing.

'You don't have to talk about it, Jessie, not if you don't want to.'

Hell, he didn't want to bring her down but she suddenly looked as if she had the weight of the world on her shoulders and he wanted to lift it off. Bring back her smile, her coquettish ease…

She cocked her head, pushed the sunglasses back onto her head as she eyed him with open curiosity. 'Does this happen to you often? People offloading their troubles on you as soon as they meet you?'

Never. Not when they knew who he was, what he'd lost…maybe that's why he felt so comfortable with her, why he wanted to delve deeper, get to know her for as long as this accidental charade could last.

He gave an impish smile, a tiny shrug. 'You can call me Aunt Joel if it helps.'

Her mouth curved up, her laughter as sweet as the sun the approaching clouds hadn't yet reached. 'Agony Aunt Joel. I love it.'

'Good.' He relaxed into the role, stretching out his legs beside hers and freeing her from his gaze. 'Now shoot...'

He waited patiently for her to speak, and when she did her voice was soft, withdrawn, the sadness returning... 'My mum was in an accident a few years back, she was hurt pretty bad...'

His chest contracted and he gave her a swift look, some memory trying to work its way to the surface...something Brendan had said... 'I'm sorry.'

'Me too.' Her smile was weak. 'I left my job and my place in the city to move home and take care of her. I didn't really think about it, I just did it. She needed me, and between my sister and me, well, she had the bigger career, greater commitments, so it made sense that I did it.'

'Is your father not...?'

She laughed, sounding harsh, bitter. 'I haven't seen him since I was six and believe me that's no bad thing. They only ever argued, Mum and him. My sister, Hannah, is ten years older than me and she'd try to joke over them, make a ton of noise, protect me, but I heard. I wasn't stupid... And I saw the bruises.'

He swallowed, the discomfort in his chest burrowing deeper as the same two words came out. 'I'm sorry.'

She shrugged. 'It's ancient history. He left and then it was just the three of us. Kind of perfect.'

'I can imagine.' Though could he really when his home life had been idyllic by comparison? A mum and dad, content together. Siblings that could just be, while he'd had to grow up fast with the responsibility of being the eldest, the heir apparent…it beat what she described by a long shot though.

'I suppose I felt like I owed it to Hannah to take care of Mum, just like Hannah had taken care of me for so long.'

He nodded, his jaw pulsing as he fought to relax it. 'How is your mum now?'

Her eyes misted over and he mentally cursed himself, realising too late he already knew the answer as the brain fog cleared and he recollected the conversation he'd had with Brendan a few months back. When her sister had taken a very rare chunk of leave from work and Brendan had been chipping in on her cases.

'She died, six months ago.' Her voice rasped, her breath juddering through her. 'She had a seizure. There was nothing I could do.'

No. And he shouldn't have pressed her on it. Brought her so much pain. Why did he have to be so useless? So thoughtless?

'I'm sorry,' he repeated, helpless, angry. He itched to reach for her, to offer her physical comfort, anything to help, but would she welcome it when he was no more than a stranger? Worse still, he wasn't who she thought he was. 'I really am.'

She sniffed, gave a delicate shrug as she picked at some grass at her feet. 'It was a relief to have her no longer in pain, but I'd give anything to tell her that I love her again. To hear her laugh or bollock me, anything to feel normal again.'

Her words struck a chord within him, silencing his voice, holding him captive.

'I don't know whether it's because I spent so long filling my days caring for her, throwing my focus into making sure she had everything she needed, that now she's gone I'm—I'm lost...or if I'll always feel this way because she is gone.' Jessie lifted her eyes to his, the confusion in her vulnerable depths hammering his own feelings home. 'Does that make sense?'

'Yes.' His affirmation was husky, raw in the face of her pain and acknowledging his own.

Her eyes narrowed, her voice a whisper. 'You've lost someone too?'

He wasn't surprised that she'd worked it out. Exposed beneath her watchful gaze, uncomfortable in the knowledge that he never spoke of it with anyone, and yet here, with this woman he hardly knew—this warm-hearted, honest, and open woman—he had the desire to spill his guts and be done with it.

'My father died...'

Your father and your wife, your life…

But he couldn't talk about Katie, not without baring his soul, and he wasn't ready for that, likely never would be.

'It was unexpected. A heart attack while away on business. One minute he was here, the next…'

And the next your life was turned on its head and you sold your soul to the devil working to replace him, working so hard you neglected the most important person in the world to you…

'You never got to say goodbye…'

Sympathy and pity glistened in her gaze but their presence didn't bring the usual sting, the unease, the need to make a quick exit before it choked him inside out.

'And you did.' He brushed off his thighs. 'I don't think it makes it any easier.'

'I guess…but even then, there are things I wish I'd said.' Her eyes didn't leave him. 'What about you?'

'Were there things I wished I'd said?'

She nodded, her head doing that little tilt that exposed the delicate arch to her neck, the pulse point he had the urge to tease with his lips…the thought far more entertaining than the difficult terrain they'd hit on.

But he owed her this—the same truth that she had gifted him.

'I was the eldest, shaped to follow in my father's shoes, I was a mini-him. I don't think there's much I didn't know about him or vice versa. He was proud of me and, though he was never one to say it, he loved us in his own way... I think...'

She gave a perplexed smile. 'You *think*?'

His laugh was strained. 'Okay, I know. But he was a hard man to please, an even harder man to wring any sentiment from. He was a man of his generation, not one to wear his heart on his sleeve.'

His death though...his death had exacerbated everything. Made Joel the man he had become, a workaholic paying no heed to what was going on beyond the office walls. A mirror image of his father.

'What about your mother, is she still...?'

He nodded. 'Very much alive and very much the mother hen.' Guilt tugged at the smile he tried to give. His mother's current clucking very much the result of his own actions. Actions he couldn't see a way to change. 'She was devastated after Dad died, but we rallied around, my brothers, my sister...we took care of her. My sister more than us men, we're not...well, I guess we're all like Dad, stereotypical blokes, not quite in tune with our softer side.'

She smiled at that, leaning in to nudge him with her bare shoulder, skin brushing skin, heat brushing heat as the spark ignited between them, catching at his breath.

'Oh, I don't think you're all that out of tune.' Her voice was soft, her eyes softer still. Was she thinking the same...feeling the same?

'No?' he murmured.

'No.' Her lashes lowered. 'Agony Aunt Joel sort of becomes you.'

He choked on a laugh, gruff, tight. '*Please* never let anyone else hear you call me that. I have a reputation to uphold.'

Her brows lifted. 'A reputation?'

He swept a hand over his front. 'Do I look like a softie to you?'

He expected her to laugh, expected her to break the connection…only she *did* look and, judging by the banked desire in her gaze, she liked what she saw.

'Not in the slightest, but I'd put money on you being very much a walnut.'

'A *what*?' He laughed wholeheartedly now…of all the things he'd been called before, never had he been deemed a walnut. And it was the last thing he'd expected to come out of her mouth when all he could think of was kissing it.

'I guess you haven't heard Muhammad Ali's analogy before…?'

'I can't say I have, but I'm all ears now.'

She grinned. 'He used fruit and nuts to describe people and their personalities.'

'Did he, now?' He sounded as if he was teasing but he wasn't. He was getting more and more enraptured by the second. 'So, what does a walnut say about me?'

'Well, as a walnut, you're hard on the outside and soft on the inside.'

'Right, okay.' He pressed his lips together with a nod. 'And what, pray tell, are the others?'

'There's the pomegranate—obviously.'

He chuckled. 'Obviously. Which is…?'

'Hard on the outside *and* the inside.'

He pressed his lips back together, not quite believing what he was hearing but loving it all the same.

'Then there's the prune—soft on the outside, hard on the inside.'

'Walnut. Pomegranate. Prune.' He nodded. 'What's last?'

'Me.'

He smiled softly. 'You.'

She pressed her palm to her chest and with mock sincerity said, 'I am a grape.'

'Grape?'

'Soft on the outside and…'

'Soft on the inside,' he completed for her, their eyes locked, his heart beating wildly in his chest. His head had known she was off-limits, his best friend had made that perfectly clear, but now…his heart knew it too. She *was* soft. Too soft for him. Too nice. Too warm. Too much of everything that made his body come alive…

He cleared his throat. 'I'm not sure about this whole fruit and nut analogy. I'd rather be the sheep in wolf's clothing.'

'Don't worry, the great Ali said he was a walnut too. It didn't ruin his image.'

'You sure about that? A wrinkly walnut is hardly the stuff of fantasies.'

She laughed, leaning forward to cup his cheek, her eyes widening on contact as though she'd surprised herself with the move—hell, she'd surprised him. His lips parted with his sharp inhalation, his pulse spiked, heat streaking through his core…

She snapped her hand back. 'Sorry, I—'

'No.' He took her wrist, pulled her back to him, encouraged her palm back to his cheek, covered it with his own. 'You just?'

She wet her lips. 'I was about to point out your lack of wrinkles.'

He smiled, his cheek shifting beneath her palm, stirring up the tingle already rife beneath her touch.

'And your skin…' he reached out, brushed his knuckles along her cheekbone '…is softer than a grape.'

She gave the tiniest of shrugs, the smallest of giggles. 'Even the great Ali can't get everything right…'

'No, and I have no idea how we've gone from grapes and walnuts to this.'

'Me neither.'

He opened up his hand, palmed her cheek, his eyes tracing her every reaction—the gentle parting of her lips, the pulse in her neck working, the lowering of her lashes… He smoothed his hand back, burying his fingers in her soft auburn hair, and had the strangest sense of being where he needed to be, where he wanted to be.

The air grew heavy, thick, the waves punctuating the loaded silence. Was she moving closer, or was he?

'So tell me, what's my secrecy worth?'

Her voice, so husky, teased at his control, but her words…her question… His brows drew together. 'Your secrecy?'

She nodded against his palm, her nose brushing against his, her delicate scent lifting on the warm sea breeze. 'Well, if I'm to keep your Agony Aunt status to myself, what's it worth?'

He wasn't smiling, he wasn't laughing. No, his head was ranting at him to put an end to this before it went too far…but…

'What would you like it to be worth?'

Bad, bad move…

Her lashes fluttered, her breath slow and shaky. 'One kiss.'

No, he hadn't imagined the connection, he hadn't imagined any of it.

He was going to hell, and there was nothing to stop him.

CHAPTER FOUR

O_H, _{MY} G_{OD}! Had she really just come out with it? So brazen and careless and...*you wanted to be wild again!*

But there was wild and there was stupid and—

His lips touched hers, the lightest of sweeps, and her brain stopped, her body reacted...rusty but no less willing as she opened up to him, her tongue teasing out, and he groaned, low, almost pained. 'You taste better than any grape too.'

She breathed in his words, felt her lips curve against his mouth. 'And I hate walnuts.'

His groan became a rakish laugh, his hands lowering to her waist as he threw her over him in one deft move that left her breathless and disorientated...or was that his kiss? She didn't care. Only that she didn't want this to stop. This heady feeling that promised a release so powerful it could wipe out the pain of the last few years...for this moment at least.

'But I don't hate you,' she murmured as she straddled him, combing her hands through his hair and grasping for the wildness buried within.

She'd asked for one kiss, but one could be deep and unrelenting, couldn't it?

Especially when he wanted her too. The evidence of his arousal, thick between her legs, his breaths as short and shallow as her own…his scent was of the sea, of his shower, his taste was of the recent mango juice and something else…something luscious and carnal and utterly additive. And she wanted more, so much more.

No matter how unwise, how unsafe, how ill-advised…though how could it hurt when it was temporary and fitted so perfectly with her new-found plan? Hannah wanted her to be reborn and she was willing to bet Joel had the power to do it.

'This is crazy,' she rasped, between kisses. Crazy, but she wasn't about to stop. New Jessie was taking all he was willing to give…for the pleasure and the explosive memories their connection promised.

'You got that right.'

'But I don't want to stop.'

'You got that right too.'

His tongue delved into her mouth deeper, more desperate, and she melted, her whimper as unrestrained as she felt.

The wind picked up around them, its force in sync with their frenzied movement, their hands raking over one another, teeth clashing as they lost all control.

He clutched her behind to draw her closer, tore his mouth away to press his forehead to her chest. 'But—we need to.'

She shifted over him, shook her head, disorientated by the sudden change, disappointment threatening to rob her of her plan, her fresh confidence, the new Jessie she wanted to cling to now she'd started. 'We don't. We really don't.'

He sucked in a ragged breath, shook his head as he looked up at her. 'Look, we—'

'Joel? Jessie?'

They froze, their heads snapping in the direction of the voice.

Oh, God! Anton!

She scurried back, folding her arms in the hope they'd conceal the way her nipples prickled beneath her vest top like beacons.

Anton cleared his throat, his eyes trained on a spot above their heads. 'I'm sorry to interrupt but Mr Hart is asking for you.'

'For me?' She frowned, pressing her hand to her throat as she wished her pulse would stop pounding there. 'But—'

'No, *you...*' Anton looked to Joel, his brows arching in obvious disapproval. Oh, God, she really was going to get the guy fired.

'Please, Anton, this isn't—' she started as Joel shot to his feet.

'I'll call him now,' he interjected, a hand raking through his hair as he sent her the briefest of looks, his expression indecipherable, though the colour in his cheeks said it all.

'He's on his mobile I take it?' he asked Anton,

his voice surprisingly in control now, his presence too. How could a guy caught in the act, his job in jeopardy, be so…autocratic?

'Yes.'

Anton nodded and Joel gave her a smile that smacked of regret. 'It was lovely to meet you, Jessie. I'm sorry that I have to say goodbye.'

Goodbye?

Why did that sound so final? Surely, if he thought he was fired he wouldn't be so chilled out about it. And if he wasn't fired then he'd still be here tomorrow and the day after that and the day after that. Working here and…maybe befriending her? Helping her get out of this funk so she could return home all the better for it. It wasn't as if she couldn't achieve it on her own, of course not, but she had to admit, he was the one who'd sparked the sudden urgency to achieve it.

The sudden urgency to take all the fun life had to offer, no regrets.

'Are you okay?' Concerned blue eyes penetrated hers and she realised, rather belatedly, that they were all waiting on her to respond.

She forced a smile, swept her hand over the back of her neck. 'Of course… I just—I hope everything's okay…with you?'

The unsaid apology was clear. That she was sorry she had put him in a tricky spot. She was sorry that she might have got him into trouble. She was sorry, not sorry to have had her body feel something again. Something incredible and intense and all-consuming.

'Absolutely, it is. Anton will see you back to the house, won't you, Anton?'

Anton nodded, and if he was bothered by Joel's commanding air and role reversal he didn't show it.

'But I *will* see you later?' She wanted it to be rhetorical, but…

'I'll see what I can do.'

His gaze lingered a second longer, a second *too* long judging by the brows threatening to escape Anton's hairline now, but it gave her the reassurance she needed.

He still wanted her and she most certainly wanted him.

'You're supposed to be airborne,' was the greeting he got from Brendan as soon as the line connected.

'And you're supposed to be working. Can't all be on best behaviour today, can we?'

'Joel, seriously, whatever's going on in Tokyo, Simon wants you there.'

'Simon wants me there so he can lay eyes on me for the first time in months. That's all.'

'And is that so bad?'

'It is when it comes with the emotional blackmail sure to ensue…'

'Is it blackmail when they're only speaking the truth?'

Joel blew out a breath, using his frustration to tamp down the guilt. 'Look, the business is fine, the great Austin empire doesn't need me to keep it ticking along, and my brothers need to get used to working without me. They've done well enough so far.'

'And as you've already pointed out, it's not all about the business. Your sister wants you at her engagement party—I think she's worried you won't show.'

'I'll be there.'

'Will you, because you haven't RSVP'd and the deadline was—?'

'As her brother, I hardly think I need to RSVP.'

'When that brother is you, you do.'

'Jesus, Brendan, if I say I'll be there, I'll be there.'

'Can you even remember when it is?'

'Yes.' He couldn't but he wasn't about to admit it. He still had the invite somewhere in his possession…

'I'm going to pretend I believe you.'

'Gee, thanks, bro. Want to insult me over something else or can I get back to packing?'

'You said you were already packed.'

Busted. 'So I did…'

'And Anton tells me you've been showing Jessie around…'

Joel grimaced, the guilt resurfacing with force. 'I might have been.'

'How is she?'

Joel frowned at the phone, making sure he was

still connected to Brendan, the same Brendan that had told him in no uncertain terms to avoid her like the plague. Was Brendan now pitying him too, softening in an attempt to draw him out? Well, screw that.

'Right, back up a step. Who are you and what have you done with my best friend, who only a few hours ago ordered me to stay away from her?'

'It's called giving you the benefit of the doubt and assuming you ran into each other and had no choice but to be civil…'

There was civil and then there was kissing her…and that kiss…it fired through his veins even now. Feeding his guilt and holding his tongue.

'Joel?'

'Of course I was civil.'

'And now you can leave, right?'

'Yes.' Not that he wanted to. He hadn't wanted to before and now he wanted to even less. There was something about Jessie that he could lose himself in. Her fresh-faced honesty, her heart that she wore so blatantly on her sleeve, and those lips…

'Joel. *Joel…?*'

He was losing himself now and she wasn't even here. 'What?'

'Are you even listening?'

'Of course I'm listening.'

'Then why, when I told you that Paolo was bringing the Jeep around to take you to the airport, did you say nothing?'

'I wasn't aware there was something I should say.'

'Thank you might be nice.'

'Thank you, Brendan.'

'Don't be facetious.'

'Then stop mothering me.'

'I don't want to mother you, Joel, I just want my mate back.'

'And airborne before sunset.'

'You know flights are grounded after dark and that storm isn't going to hang around waiting for you to leave.'

'Yeah, yeah, I know.' Through the clearing ahead he could make out Paolo sitting at the wheel of the estate's Jeep, bopping to his music, and he wanted to slap himself for being such a selfish idiot. 'Jokes aside, Brendan, thank you for letting me stay.'

'Any time.'

Less than an hour later, having checked the villa for any stray belongings, he was en route to the airport, a chatty Paolo at the wheel, his head on his destination. Maybe a short stint in Miami wouldn't go amiss. Plenty to do. Plenty to see. Plenty to distract himself further.

It won't have a Jessie though...

No, that woman was one of a kind, and he hadn't even got to say goodbye. Not properly.

One explosive kiss and it was over before it had ever really begun.

Doesn't stop you looking her up...it's not like you don't know who she is and how to reach her...

And face the wrath of Brendan and her sister...?

The smallest of smiles teased at his lips. Jessie would be worth it, for sure. But she was too good, too kind, too sensitive for a man like him.

He sighed. No, she was better off free of his tease.

'That Jessie sure is something, don't you reckon, Mr A?'

He glanced across at Paolo. Was the man reading his mind? 'What do you know—?'

A loud boom reverberated through the Jeep, startling them straight. Paolo cursed, his knuckles whitening around the steering wheel as the vehicle swerved out beneath them.

'Hold on, Mr A!' he shouted over the rattling cabin, the whooshing of the deflating tyre sickeningly unmistakable.

'I'm holding all right.' Joel gripped the grab handle and stared straight ahead—the narrow dirt road, the cliff face and the sharp drop into the ocean alternating as the car spun out. His stomach threatened to empty and he clenched his teeth, squeezed his eyes shut...

He'd said he was going to hell...he just hadn't anticipated it would be so soon.

Are you settled? Is the place as amazing as it sounds?

Jessie smiled at Hannah's message, feeling far more comfortable with her surroundings now that she'd found something of an ally in Joel. Someone on her level who she could talk to, spend time with…lose her inhibitions with. She pressed her lips together.

Okay, maybe she was getting carried away. There might be rules, for one. Rules that prohibited him from spending time with her. But then, would he have acted so in control when Anton had appeared if there were?

The more she thought about it, the more she doubted it, but the only way to know for sure was to ask and the only person safe to ask was Joel himself. And for that she'd have to wait until she saw him again.

She wanted to laugh at her own behaviour, as out of character as it was, but then, she was having fun. Pure, unadulterated fun, and that was why replying to Hannah was easy.

Typing out a swift and effusive response, she tossed her phone on the bed and turned to eye the outdoors that had darkened through the course of the day, the sky growing heavy, the winds picking up.

Anton had assured her, just as Joel had assured her, it was nothing to worry about. A bit of wind, maybe some rain, maybe some lightning…all things she was accustomed to at home.

She checked her watch and smoothed her palms over the little black dress she'd chosen to wear. It felt a tad OTT for dining alone, but in surroundings such as these dressing anything less than best felt wrong.

With the tiniest flicker of hope that she might see Joel en route, she headed for the dining room. The tantalising scent of spices, rich and warm, reached her, their aroma enough to set her stomach rumbling.

Food had become more of a necessity than a pleasure the last few years. Cooking for herself and her mum, it had lost its magic when Mum hadn't been able to stomach anything too complex. Bland and simple had been the way, sticking to regular mealtimes and sitting together, more for companionship than nourishment.

And the last six months had been strange. Eating alone, no desire or inclination to do something different for herself. She'd been stuck in a rut, cooking the same old meals, freezing up batches…

Now here she was in the lap of luxury, about to sit at a table so beautifully decorated she wished she'd brought her phone just to snap a picture of it for Hannah. Even her unsentimental sister would appreciate the beauty of the red hibiscus and yellow buttercups creating a trail around two lit hurricane lamps, their colours vibrant against the rich, dark wood.

'Ah, Jessie, are you ready to eat?' Anton seemed to appear from nowhere, seamlessly stepping into the room with a warm smile and polite nod.

'Positively ravenous, Anton.' She pressed a hand to her growling stomach. 'I'm surprised you can't hear my belly rumbling from over there.'

He chuckled. 'May I?'

He pulled out the chair before the single place setting that had more glasses and cutlery than she knew what to do with.

Hannah would know though.

Hannah would belong.

But you're the one here, so enjoy it!

She lowered herself into the chair. 'This is beautiful, Anton. Thank you.'

'I'm glad you approve. June loves coming up with new ideas for the centre arrangement. Can I pour you some wine?'

She gave a nervous laugh. 'That would be lovely, thank you.'

She took up the glass already filled with water and took a sip as Anton poured the wine, her gaze drifting to the outdoors. To the rocky pond filled with koi, waterlilies and papyrus and the distant palms that were shifting in the escalating winds.

Visually the change in the weather was obvious, but she could hear none of it over the gentle instrumental music playing through an invisible sound system. Money clearly bought you amazing soundproofing, though it was odd to see the rising chaos outside and feel none of it inside.

If only it was possible to feel that way as a person…disconnected and unaffected by the outside world…

'Please don't worry, Jessie. We really will be fine.'

Grateful that he'd misinterpreted whatever he'd seen in her face, she nodded.

'It is starting to look quite menacing out there…'

Which brought her to her next concern: where did Joel sleep? Were the staff quarters part of the main house or in the grounds somewhere or close by? Was he, right now, securing his own house against the elements?

'It'll pass. A few days and then we will be back to blue skies and calmer seas.'

She put on a smile and he left, returning promptly with a steaming bowl in hand.

'For the starter tonight Vittorio has made a local favourite, callaloo soup. It has a spiced coconut-milk base with diced pumpkin, okra, pimento peppers and crab meat. It's sure to satisfy that stomach of yours *and* calm the nerves.'

She breathed in the scented steam as he lowered it before her. 'It smells delicious.'

And ignoring the tiniest gripe that she didn't deserve all this fuss, she tucked in.

Spices danced on her flavour-starved tongue and she barely suppressed a moan. A task that became harder with each mouthful, and no sooner had she set her cutlery down than the next course arrived—grilled chicken with a pineapple salsa—and the next, the final and utterly scrumptious dessert, a *pudín de pan*. Caribbean bread pudding, Anton told her.

She ate every last morsel, refusing to stop even when her stomach protested.

'Please tell Vittorio that was the best meal I've had in years, if not ever,' she told Anton as he cleared her last dish away.

'You'll make his day. Can I get you anything else this evening—would you like a drink in the bar perhaps?'

She laughed, the idea as alien as it was appealing. 'I guess I should try and stay awake a little longer.'

'A rum before bed? A cocktail or...?'

'A hot chocolate?' she suggested hesitantly, relaxing as he smiled.

'Of course.'

He didn't need to tell her he wasn't accustomed to such a request and she didn't care if it made her sound like a child—her sleep was fitful enough without adding more alcohol to the mix.

Though maybe the alcohol would knock her out so completely that the dreams and night sweats wouldn't come...

'Maybe a splash of rum in the hot chocolate wouldn't go amiss.'

His grin widened. 'Certainly! It is the Caribbean way.'

CHAPTER FIVE

'I'M SORRY, MR A.'

Paolo swiped the sweat from his brow and sat back on his haunches, frowning at the fresh tyre they'd managed to fit, having spent a fair amount of time digging the vehicle out of the verge between the road and the cliff face.

'I think the fates have decided you're stuck with us a bit longer—it'll be too dark for your flight to take off now and that storm is going to hit overnight.'

Joel grinned as he cleaned his hands off on a rag. 'Hey, we survived with barely a scratch and the Jeep will clean up with a bit of a buff. I'd take that as a win.'

'But I know how keen you were to get away today.'

Keen? Joel wouldn't put it like that but setting Paolo straight wouldn't help the guilt etched in the young man's face. Learning that it was the guy paying his wages who was keen to see Joel gone would only stress him out further...

'There are far worse places in this world to get stuck.' Joel tossed the rag in the back of the Jeep. 'Right, come on, I owe you a beer.'

Paolo gave a surprised laugh. 'What for?'

'For a God-awful afternoon, all because you were lumped with the task of taking me to the airport.'

'That's my job.'

Joel shrugged. 'Makes no odds to me—you lost an afternoon, I missed a flight, and I'd say we could both do with a drink.'

'Wouldn't you rather I got you back to the villa?'

'And face Anton's panic when he realises he has an extra guest to host for a day or two?'

Not to mention the fact that Anton would let Brendan know and then Brendan would be on at him.

And then there was Jessie...

How would she feel about sharing her space for a day or two?

His body warmed as his mind conjured her up with effortless ease, their heated kiss quick to follow...yup, far better to stay away from that temptation a little while longer.

'That's a good point.' Paolo straightened, tugging his phone from his back pocket. 'I'll call Anton now, give him the heads-up so June can sort a room for you tonight.'

Joel nodded. He could hardly stop Paolo from doing his job...perhaps he could feign poor mobile reception when the inevitable call from Brendan came. Storms did that, after all.

'But are you sure about the drink?' Paolo scratched the back of his head. 'I don't think I've ever been invited for a drink with a guest before.'

'There's a first time for everything.'

'I'm not sure how Anton will take it.'

Joel held up his hands. 'Far be it from me to get you in trouble but I don't plan on telling anyone if you don't...besides, I'd much prefer to have a drinking buddy than go it alone. And I can hardly drive if I have more than one, so if anyone asks, you're my designated driver.'

'Well, when you put it like that...' Paolo's smile lifted to one side. 'Basil's Bar?'

'Basil's is perfect. And it's taco and tequila night...we have to eat, right?' Food *and* drinks ought to keep him out of trouble long enough for the villa to be asleep on his return and he could deal with the fallout tomorrow...along with the storm. 'Ask Anton to let me know which room I'm in—that way I don't have to disturb anyone when we return.'

'Will do. And I'll let him know you'll have eaten to save Vittorio from a hissy fit thinking he has to feed you last-minute.'

Joel laughed, loving that Paolo was loosening up a little and dropping the respectful distance and quiet mouth.

'A high-end chef having a hissy fit...who'd have thought it?'

Paolo laughed with him. 'I reckon we have a good few hours before those clouds hit in earnest and these roads become a river.'

'Then we'll have to make sure we're back long before then.'

'Yes, boss.'

'No boss, just Joel.'

'No can do, Mr A.'

And just like that he was back on his miserable pedestal...

It's pitch-black and cold. Oh, so cold. Something's pressing on my chest...something heavy and damp. I open my mouth to breathe but there's no air, no space. I grip my throat, my eyes watering. I'm choking on nothing, my voice stolen by the dark vacuum I'm in, and then I hear it. Scratching. Nails against earth, against wood...

'Help!'

I try to scream but what comes out is too quiet, too hoarse.

'Help!'

The tiniest glimmer of light breaks through, cold air sweeps over my skin. I suck in a breath. And another. It's tainted by dirt and something else. Something chilling...

Death.

'Jessie, sweetheart...it's all okay. It's just a dream. Wake up. Wake up.'

'Mum!'

Jessie bolted upright in bed, one hand clutching at her throat, the other clenched in the bed sheets.

'Mum...' A pained whisper into the empty room, a room she didn't recognise...the chill of the air-conditioning against her sweat-drenched skin as unfamiliar as the floral scent in the air. She shuddered, her brain struggling to play catch-up.

And then it comes with sickening force, the chilling reminder: *Mum's gone and there's no comfort here.*

She balled her fists, nails biting into her palms as she cursed the dream that had haunted her childhood, and in the past few years had returned with a vengeance. The sensation of being trapped, suffocated, buried alive...

Back then it would be her mother's soothing hand on her brow, her mum's soft, familiar voice that would rouse her, comfort her...

A sob racked her body, grief mixing with the fear still ripe in her veins.

Why were dreams such torture? To live within them, to feel the horror, to believe...and then to wake, and for a moment everything feels safe, as it was...only it's not.

Mum's gone and no dream, no amount of wishing, could change that.

Anxiety built like a twisting coil inside her, shortening her breaths, stabbing at her insides...

Adam had initially tried to calm her like Mum once had, with the odd word, the odd hair-stroke, but he'd soon tired of being startled awake, drenched in her sweat, having received a slapped cheek or a kick to the thigh, exhausted and cranky from another broken night as he'd take himself off to another room. If only it had ended there, his way of dealing with it. Private. Between them.

Pain ripped through her and she clamped her jaw shut.

Don't think of it now, Jessie. He's gone. It doesn't matter any more. Relax. Count...

She forced a slow breath and another, her eyes trying to focus through the dark as she fought to ground herself in the present...

What she could feel—the soft mattress beneath her, the smooth Egyptian cotton sheets. What she could smell—the spa-like scent of the villa with its floral accents designed to soothe. What she could see—the rain tracing moonlit patterns across the floor as it trickled down the glass...

Rain! Typical! The tension slid from her body as she clung to the sight.

Come to paradise, they said...it'll be glorious, they said...

When in reality she'd only succeeded in bringing the great British weather with her...

Though torrential rain beat a hurricane any day of the week.

Tugging her chemise away from her skin, she padded to the window and touched her hand to the cool glass. Stared out at the swaying palms, the moon and the racing clouds above, the rain beating ripples into the surface of her private pool.

This *was* paradise...a wet paradise, but paradise none the less.

She took another steadying breath, grateful to feel

her chest easing, her pulse too, and let her mind drift to Mum. Mum's caring eyes, her soothing voice, her magic remedy… A smile touched Jessie's lips. She may be a grown adult, but Mum's remedy for her night terrors was as effective now as it ever was.

Resisting the urge to turn on a light, she made her way to the kitchen as quietly as possible. The last thing she needed was to wake a member of staff and have them witness the state she was in. She didn't need to look in a mirror to know her eyes were red, her cheeks tear-stained, her hair and clothing clinging to her skin.

She pulled open the fridge, taking a moment to appreciate the cool air inside before bending down and grabbing the milk.

'Mum's answer to everything…'

A sudden noise behind her brought her up sharp, her head hitting the shelf in the door as the milk slipped in her grasp. Fumbling to save it, she spun on the spot as a man fell in through the kitchen doorway…

'Joel?'

He stumbled to a startled stop, his soaked appearance as shocking as his *actual* appearance. He looked like a drowned rat. A very sexy, slightly worse-for-wear drowned rat, his clothes sticking to his skin… The rain exposed every hard angle, every chiselled muscle. From his face to his jaw, to his abs, to his… She swallowed.

'Jessie!'

Her eyes shot back to his, her cheeks on fire, her heart still racing with a lot more than shock now. He cleared his throat, his brows disappearing behind his rain-slicked hair.

'I'm sorry, I wasn't expecting anyone to be up. Are you okay?' His hand gestured in the vague direction of her head and a bump that would likely exist come morning, and she shook her head, wanting to tell him not to worry, but her tongue failed to engage.

He scraped his hands through his hair, blew out a breath with a curse. 'I really am sorry.'

'Buy why are…? What are you…?' *Get your words out, Jessie!* 'You're soaked through!'

'And you're…' His throat bobbed, his eyes raking over her, torching her skin, his mouth opening and closing but nothing emerging. At least she wasn't alone in her ineptitude to speak. She'd blame the late hour, if not for the way he was looking at her…those eyes…during the day they'd been as blue as the sea, now they were dark, seductive, glittering with so much—

So much that you shouldn't act on but want to all the same.

'I was in bed,' she said simply. 'Asleep.' *Obviously.* 'I woke up and fancied a drink.'

Oh, it just gets better and better…

She raised the milk in her hand with a hapless smile, an embarrassed shrug, and silently cursed.

Why couldn't she have been getting something a little more sophisticated?

His eyes drifted to the milk and then back again, following her arm to her chest and the chemise that was clinging to her very damp and very pert...

'Crap!'

'Huh?' His eyes launched to hers.

'Huh?'

'You said crap...?'

'I did?'

A smile teased at his lips. 'Uh-huh.'

Tugging at the hem of her shorts as though it would somehow make a difference to their skimpy length, she confessed, 'These weren't meant for seeing.'

'What weren't?'

His eyes danced as he stepped closer and her pulse skipped, the cool air from the fridge chilling the backs of her bare thighs as her front basked in the heat of him. The scent of his body mixed up with the rain, earth and beer titillated her senses... And why was that even sexy?

'You've been drinking?' Oh, God, now she sounded as if she were scolding him when in reality *she* was scalding, her words hot with her embarrassment, her body fired with desire. Maybe it was the lateness of the hour, the shock of his being here, the state of clothing—on both their parts.

He gave a choked laugh. 'Is that a problem? I know I look pretty good for my age but no one can mistake me for being underage.'

'Are you allowed to drink when you're working?'

He's not working right now, you idiot!

His grin widened. 'I'm off the clock.'

Her cheeks burned deeper, her eyes widening a fraction more. 'Of course you are.'

'So, you were saying?'

'I was saying what?'

She sucked in a breath which froze in her lungs as he reached out...but he kept on going, bypassing her for the fridge door as he swung it closed behind her.

'Best not let *all* the cold air out...' Now they were almost chest to chest, and without the chill of the fridge she was burning up inside *and* out. 'You were saying, *these* weren't meant for seeing...'

His eyes were fixed on hers, penetrating her every thought and making her crave all that she shouldn't.

But you're going to be a little wild, remember, live a little, crave all you like.

'What did you mean by "these"?'

She wet her lips. 'My pyjamas.'

One brow lifted a fraction. 'Why?'

'Because—because look at them.'

'Oh, I have...and I daren't look any more.'

She swallowed a grimace. 'That bad?'

'No, Jessie.' The slightest shake of his head. 'Unless you mean bad as in the very, very good kind...'

Her lips parted, her heart leapt. Say something clever, something flirtatious, something...anything...

Was she really so out of practice?

His eyes dipped in spite of his words. 'Is there a pair of shorts under there or just…?'

'*Yes*, there's a pair of shorts!'

He chuckled at her fluster as she raised a hand to sweep a hair that had caught on her lip back behind her ear, and his blazing eyes tracked the movement, their depths revealing so much and yet nothing at all.

'I should leave you to your milk.'

'My milk…?'

He dragged in a breath that seemed to pain him, a step back that seemed to pain him further, and took the said milk from her limp grasp.

'I take it you want a glass.'

'I did.' But she didn't any more. She wanted him, in all his rain-drenched glory. And the kitchen counter felt as good a place as any.

Jessie!

Now, that sounded like her mother in her head, berating her daring thoughts. In reality, it was her own weak conscience telling her to stop it, but hell, this was her plan, to be brave, to be bold, to *dare*…

So she gave him a smile as sultry as she could muster and gestured to the milk. 'Fancy joining me?'

'For a milk?' His eyes sparkled in the moonlight and she laughed softly, her confidence growing with the butterflies in her stomach, the molten heat swirling just beneath.

'I hate drinking alone.'

He stared at her a second longer, those dark eyes

burning into her… 'Well, when you put it like that… far be it from me to say no.'

The thrill of triumph, of excitement, had her floating on air as she turned to pull two glasses off the shelf, delaying her return as she closed her eyes for a moment's calm before turning back and—

'Oh!' She found herself chest to damp torso, wide eyes to a throat that was showing signs of a five o'clock shadow and his scent… She almost sighed with her inhalation. 'You really do move very quietly.'

His chuckle was low. 'The price one pays for being the eldest and being told not to wake the baby several times over… Allow me.'

He placed the milk on the counter behind her, took the glasses from her next, his body brushing against hers, and she shivered. 'Are you cold?'

'Hardly.' She looked up into his eyes that were a crazy mix of desire and concern. 'But you must be— wet clothes and this villa's air-con don't mix well.'

'I haven't noticed.'

'No?'

'No.' It was a murmur from his lips that were inches from hers and she couldn't tug her eyes from their fullness, the way they parted ever so slightly as he looked at her, the hint of tongue as he wet them. She wanted to kiss him, could see the reciprocal desire blazing back at her.

'Jessie…?'

'Yes.'

CHAPTER SIX

THE MOONLIGHT THROUGH the window gave her skin an alabaster glow as she lifted her gaze to his. Eyes, big and round and dark with longing, stared up at him.

She looked ethereal, almost mythical, and no force on earth could have stopped him from asking and taking…

'May I?'

Her lashes fluttered, her body swaying towards him. 'Yes.'

And he didn't hesitate. He claimed her with such ferocity, she gasped against his lips, his own growl guttural and as unleashed as he suddenly felt.

Her mouth was sweet, her moan sweeter still. She reached into his hair, curved her entire body into him—warm silk and pliable skin against cool, wet cotton and hard muscle. A contrast that shouldn't work, a contrast that should have jarred her back and away from him. Instead, it heightened every sense, made it more illicit…her heat, her scent, her delicate frame as it fitted so perfectly against his.

He raked his hands down her sides, hungry to explore every inch, exposed or otherwise. 'You're like a little night nymph, sent to seduce me.'

Her laugh was throaty. 'I like the sound of that.' Her nip to his lip both daring and surprising. Where had the coquettish girl of moments before gone, the one concerned with her skimpy attire, or the one who had struggled to say a word when he'd shaken her hand that morning?

He didn't know, and right now he didn't care. He wanted the whole, contradictory mix.

He let her back him up to the kitchen surface, her strength belying her slight frame, and then he spun them at the last second, lifting her up until she was perched on its edge.

'You're too damned appealing, Jessie Rose. Whether you're being coy or flirtatious, skimpy pyjamas or no...'

'And you need to get out of yours before you catch yourself a chill.'

Desire choked up his laugh as she slipped her hand beneath his shirt, ran her nails over his skin. 'I'm not wearing pyjamas.'

'Details. Details,' she murmured between kisses.

'How is it possible that you're turning me on while mothering me?'

'How is it possible you have me behaving like some harlot on night one?' she threw back.

'Are you suggesting this isn't how you normally behave?' He'd surmised as much but still...

She punished him with another nip to his lip and a playful shove. 'Absolutely not.'

'Well, that makes two of us...' He tugged her

back, kissing her deeply as one hand slipped beneath her top and she gave the most delectable whimper, her skin prickling to greet his touch.

'Maybe we should take this to my room,' she rasped against his lips. 'I'd hate for anyone to walk in.'

'Everyone's asleep.'

'I was asleep all of ten minutes ago. Things change and I don't want to get you fired.'

'Fired…why would I…?'

He cursed. His job. His occupation. The one she thought he had. Sanity came crashing down with debilitating force. This wasn't okay. None of it was.

'What's wrong?' She frowned at his frozen form, one skimpy strap lowered to her elbow, one full breast on tantalising show. 'Joel?'

'I'm sorry, Jessie.' He squeezed his eyes shut to her appeal, pressed his forehead to hers as he dragged in a breath. 'We shouldn't be—*I* shouldn't be doing this.'

'Why? What did I say? Is it the job?'

He backed away as though stung, shaking his head.

'Joel?' She pushed off the side, closing the distance he'd created, trying to get into his line of sight, but he wouldn't let her.

'I don't work here!' he rushed out before anything could get in the way again.

'I don't—you what?' He could hear the confusion in her tone, sense her frown. 'But you were working, today, earlier… I thought…'

His eyes found hers on impulse, guilt chewing him up inside. But this hadn't been his fault. He hadn't intended to mislead her. And he certainly hadn't told her he was employed here. She'd assumed and he hadn't corrected her.

Which was hardly any better...

'I know what you thought.' He rubbed the back of his neck, ignoring the inner voice and attempting a smile that he hoped she would deem apologetic enough. 'I'm sorry. I should have set you straight, but the opportunity never presented itself and—'

'Hang on...' She raised a hand to cut him off, tugged her strap into place and pinned him with her stare. 'If you don't work here and yet you *are* here, who exactly are you?'

He raked his teeth over his lower lip, held her eye. 'A guest.' Her brows nudged up, her eyes widening. 'Or I was until your arrival...at which point I was supposed to leave to make way for you, but then we had a blow-out in the Jeep which took us down a ditch, and by the time we got back on the road it was too late for the plane to depart so Paolo and I went to Basil's for a drink and something to eat and I intended to explain myself tomorrow morning but then I came in here and...'

And breathe.

He gestured to her, his smile half-cocked. 'Need I say more?'

She was staring at him, her eyes racing with thoughts that only she was privy to. In all honesty, he thought he'd done a good job of explaining himself, even if it was a bit of a ramble, so maybe—

'Are you for *real*?'

Okay, so maybe not.

'I would have told you if I thought it was important. But you were arriving, I was leaving… what was the point?'

That sounded so much better in his head…

'The point is, you made me believe you worked here. You made me believe we were one and the same. You made me believe I could open up to you. Trust you!'

He frowned. Something about this wasn't right. They'd known each other all of a day—surely he didn't warrant *this* level of heat…and he hadn't *made* her do anything, she'd done it all on her own. The only thing he was guilty of was not correcting her…

'Look, Jessie—'

'Don't you Jessie me, Agony Aunt Joel!' She poked at his chest, her growl ferocious.

No. This was definitely about more—the fiancé she'd mentioned in passing? The abusive and absentee father? Something else…?

'Jesus, I'm such an idiot!' She threw her hands up and stalked away, head shaking as he stepped after her.

'You're not an idiot. And I truly am sorry I didn't tell you sooner. But the opportunity never arose and—'

'You had plenty of opportunity, Joel!' She rounded on him, freezing him mid-step. 'In between playing the caring confidant and sticking your tongue down my throat!'

'Whoa, whoa, whoa, sweetheart.' Fire streaked down his spine. It was one thing for her to be angry with him but it was another to suggest that he had played the caring confidant to trick her into bed. 'You were as guilty as me on that front—we both confided, we both confessed—and you were the one who *asked* for one kiss!'

She coloured further, her body quivering with her shaky breath. 'Because I didn't know who you were...who you really were!'

'What difference does it make whether I work here or not? I'm still the person you met this morning, the person you kissed just now.'

She gawped at him. 'It makes all the difference.'

'Why?'

'I wouldn't have kissed you for starters.'

He gave a soft scoff. 'So, you're happy to kiss me when you think I'm a member of staff who, let's be frank, will be under strict instructions not to fraternise with the clientele. But now that you know I'm a guest like you, you—'

'No, not *like me* at all.'

'How so?'

'I wouldn't have lied.'

'I didn't lie. I omitted to correct you.'

'Screw the semantics, Joel. You lied.'

He swallowed the bitter taste in his mouth. 'And for that, I am sorry. But now you know, we can start again.'

He offered out his hand. 'Jessie Rose. I'm Joel Austin. It's a pleasure to meet you.'

She looked at his hand, incredulous. 'You really think it's that simple?'

'Isn't it? Correct me if I'm wrong, but we got on extremely well before this, and I'd like to think we can get back to that.'

'Over my dead body…'

He folded his arms and leaned back against the counter, his eyes taking in all of her—her fury, her defensive stance… 'Necrophilia really isn't my thing, darling.'

She huffed. 'Funny, Joel. Very funny.'

'What's really going on here, Jessie?'

Her eyes speared him. 'You made a fool out of me.'

'No. I unintentionally misled you. I would *never* set out to make a fool of you.'

She lifted her chin, the defiant angle at odds with the tremor in her bottom lip. He might not be the root cause of whatever this was, but he'd triggered it and that was bad enough.

'I liked you, Joel. I liked spending time with you. I hoped we could be friends.'

'And now I've apologised, why is that so impossible?'

'Because you're not a bleeding gardener, you're a guest!'

'*And?*'

'You belong in this world, with all this luxury around you...' she flapped her hands about her '...and I don't.'

'Yet you're here?'

'Because it was gifted to me.'

'It was gifted to me too.'

Her eyes widened, a flicker of hesitation in their depths. 'You know Brendan?'

'I do.'

'How?'

'We've been best friends since we were at school together.'

She gave a harsh laugh, averting her gaze as she pressed her palms to her blazing cheeks. 'Oh, God, could this get any better?'

'What's that supposed to mean?'

'This is all I need.' She started to pace, her head shaking, her chemise strap slipping again...should he tell her? 'When Hannah learns of this, I won't live it down. She thought I was a problem before, now she'll think I'm—I'm—'

'Wait!' He forgot all about the strap. 'What's Hannah got to do with this?'

'Everything!' she threw at him, mid-pace.

'But Hannah's not here.'

'No...' she yanked her strap back up, waved her hand at him '...but you are! And when you have a good gossip with your mate Brendan, he will tell Hannah and then—'

He gave an abrupt laugh. 'You think I'm going to tell Brendan any of this?'

'Well, aren't you?'

'He's the last person I'd confess all to.'

'Really?'

'If you must know, he warned me to steer clear of you. Worried I'd lead you astray…' He raked an unsteady hand through his hair 'Seems he wasn't so far off the mark either.'

'And why in heaven's name would he do that if he's your best friend?'

He swallowed down any more lies and told her the truth. 'Because I don't have the best reputation with the opposite sex and he cares about Hannah, and you by association. He doesn't trust me with you.'

A sharp huff. 'It really does get better and better…'

He straightened his spine against her direct hit. 'Well, if it's Hannah you're worried about, she won't be learning of this through me so you can chill the hell out.'

'Don't you tell me to chill. Your type are all the same.'

'My *type*?'

'Ex-prep boys. All about the conquests and the macho talk, to hell with who gets hurt along the way, so long as you look good.'

He pressed his lips together, not quite daring

to believe what he was hearing. 'Did you just call me an ex-prep boy?'

'Well, aren't you?'

'I went to Eton with Brendan, so yes, I guess technically I am.'

'And, by your own admission, your reputation with the opposite sex is shocking.'

'I don't think I used the word "shocking"—'

'You implied it!'

'And we all know how well your assumptions have worked out so far...'

She looked as if she wanted to slap him, and he couldn't help but laugh. This was crazy. Ridiculous. And it would sting if not for the fact he knew it must stem from something in her past, some hurt...

But now he was angry too. It was one thing to lay into him, make assumptions about him, but Brendan was as good as they came, and he wouldn't stand for his friend's name being dragged through the mud with him.

'Have you quite finished?'

'No.' If she lifted her chin any higher, he'd worry her neck would snap. 'I want to know why you didn't tell me. You made me worry about your job, that I'd put you on dodgy ground with Anton, when he caught us...caught us...'

'Kissing?' he supplied for her.

'Whatever.'

'I have my reasons.'

'Which are?'

'None of your business.'

Her brows soared, her surprise obvious as she struggled for a retort.

Good. He wanted her on the back foot now.

'Don't you think I deserve the truth?'

'You did. But then you pinned me with a label, made another assumption, and you threw Brendan under the bus with me.' He stepped towards her, keen to close the gap she'd created, keener still to set her straight. 'That last move was a step too far.'

'I didn't mean to imply that Brendan was…was like that…' She wet her lips—*just you,* she might as well have said. And that *did* sting.

'Good, because I tell you now he's a *great* man. One of the most generous, kind and thoughtful human beings I've ever had the good fortune to meet. You can say what you like about me, but you leave him out of it.'

She winced, her lashes fluttering over a look very much akin to guilt. 'I'm sorry, I just—'

'You were just blinded by your own prejudice?'

She didn't confirm it, but she didn't deny it either.

'By your own admission you don't even know me, and yet the assumptions keep on coming…'

'I was angry. Angry that you sucked me in…' she waved an unsteady hand at him '…angry that you let things go so far when I didn't know the truth. Let me believe it was okay, that it was just us, here, now, with no connection to the outside world.'

He paused before her and she looked up at him, her lips parting, breath catching.

'From what I can see, it *is* just us. Here. Now.'

She leaned back against the counter, creating what space she could. 'It's not the same. It's too close to home. I'd never have kissed you if I'd known.'

'You've said that already.'

'And I meant it.'

'You sure?'

'Of course I'm sure.'

She didn't sound sure. In fact she looked downright hungry as her gaze fell to his lips, and his anger fused with desire—a fierce concoction that had him edging closer.

'Even though you know how it felt, Jessie…' His eyes raked over her face '…your mouth beneath mine, moving together. Hot and hungry. A delicious tension coiling through your limbs that promises such pleasure, such gratification.'

'You're so full of yourself,' she blustered, but her cheeks were warm with telltale lust and he chuckled low and slow.

'Tell me something I don't know.'

'You're unbelievable!'

'Deny it, then. Tell me it didn't feel that way, that you didn't want me as much as I want you.'

He'd chosen his words carefully, *want* rather than *wanted*, because there was no denying that he still wanted her. Perhaps it was the challenge she now presented, perhaps it was the appeal she'd always portrayed, but there was no denying the need thrumming hot through his veins.

'You can't say it, can you…?'

He pressed his palms into the surface either side of her, boxing her in but aware of her every movement, ready to release her if she so wanted.

'That was before I knew who you were,' she said in a whisper.

'And you still don't know who I am, little nymph, so let me put you straight. I'm Joel Austin, ex-prep boy as you so kindly put it, head of the billion-dollar empire of the same name. I have more money than one could spend in a lifetime. I could buy this island and still have change for several more…'

'Bragging doesn't help your cause.'

'I'm not bragging. I'm telling you the truth, which is what you wanted from me from the start, is it not?'

'Yes, but…'

'But what?'

'Nothing.' She gave a sharp shake of her head, her neck too delicate to conceal the rapid beat of her pulse as she arched back to hold his gaze.

'The truth is I could buy anything I wanted…' his voice rasped, the heat and his honesty suffocating as his eyes trailed over her 'A snap of my fingers almost and it'll appear.'

She wet her lips, the glossy remnants tugging at his gaze. 'Bully for you.'

'Only, the one thing I want, right now…is you.'

Her eyes flared, the excited flicker in their depths belying the words that left her luscious lips. 'Well, newsflash, billionaire prep boy, I don't want you and I'm not for sale.'

'*Ex*-prep boy.' He gave a grin full of the arrogance she accused him of. 'And I never suggested you were.'

She arched her brows. 'Really?'

'Really…' He bowed his head, bringing them closer together, her mouth so teasingly near he could feel her warm breath caress his skin. 'I was simply being honest.' A touch closer and she was so still he'd swear if not for the flare to her nostrils she'd given up breathing all together. 'No more… no less.'

Gazes locked, pulses soaring in tune, she reached up on tiptoe, her lips a hair's breadth away, bypassing his mouth for his ear…

'Well, Joel Austin…' all throaty teasing '…consider yourself heard.'

And as his head turned into her, drawn in, captivated, she dropped back abruptly, arms crossed. 'Now this average Jessie is taking herself off to bed, if you please!'

She stared pointedly at his arm blocking her path and he swallowed the chuckle that wanted to erupt, the admiration too. She played it well. But she wanted him, the flush to her skin, the nipples still thrust in his direction told him well enough.

He wasn't about to press his luck, though, or force her into admitting it.

The best things in life were worth waiting for, after all.

He raised one hand to the door, freeing her with the gesture. 'As you wish…but make no mistake, Jessie, when I want something, I get it.'

She gave a choked laugh. 'Hate to break it to you, Mr More-Money-than-Sex-Appeal, but there's a first time for everything.'

He laughed at her descriptor, more amused than he likely should be. 'I'm a patient man.'

'Well, I assume you'll be leaving come morning, so you'll be waiting a *long* time.' She headed for the door, head held high, her skimpy shorts giving him a thrill he knew she wouldn't appreciate. 'Like, for ever.'

'Oh, no…' he turned to watch her leave '…I'm not going anywhere.'

She spun on the spot, the move so sharp he thought she might topple over. 'What do you mean, you're not going anywhere?'

'For as long as the storm rages, you and I are housemates.' He couldn't prevent the smile on his lips, the challenge heating his words as he folded his arms and settled into the counter. 'Scared you won't be able to resist me?'

She shook her head, spluttered out, 'You wish!'

'Time will tell…'

'This place is big enough to avoid one another.'

'But think of the staff—you don't want to add to their burden by sticking to separate mealtimes and using more rooms, do you?'

She clenched her fists at her sides. 'You're—you're so infuriating!'

'And you're hot when you're angry.'

'If you think I'll ever let you kiss me again, Joel, you have another think coming.'

'Good. Because I very much intend for you to kiss me first.'

She baulked, pursing her lips as though she was about to erupt, stamping the ground with one foot. If he told her that the move only emphasised her assets, twin assets at that, would she murder him? Likely.

A rumble worked its way through her chest, her throat, and his mouth quirked. 'Did you just growl at me, Jessie?'

'No!'

'I don't believe you.'

'Believe what you like!' She threw her arms in the air. 'I'm going to bed.'

She stormed to the door, yanked it open.

'And for the record,' he called after her, 'I don't think there's anything average about you.'

And then she was gone, and he was smiling into the empty kitchen, feeling more fired-up than he'd felt in years.

Why, the unbelievable, arrogant, chauvinistic, cocky, self-assured, lying...

Jessie stormed into her bedroom, the rant coming thick and fast as her body pleaded with her to go back and—and—slap him—kiss him—all of the above.

And give him what he wants?

'Hell, no!'

She closed her door, not as hard as she'd like but hard enough to make herself feel a smidgen better. The more distance and barriers between them the better.

How *dared* he tell her how she felt?

How *dared* he assume to know what she wanted?

How *dared* he lie to her?

No, not lie. He was right there. He'd merely failed to correct her incorrect assumption. Prejudiced. *Her?*

Well, you were, came the little voice in her head and she cursed.

He deserved it, though. He'd upset her, played her for a fool.

And so much for her anonymity and letting go without any judgement…

Could she really trust him not to say anything to Brendan? Not to boast of it and laugh at her stupidity too. It was what Adam would have done.

And there was the true cause of her anger, her upset, her hurt. Adam.

She leaned back against the door, her palms pressed flat to the wood as she tried to fend off the pain, the shortened breaths that would only lead to another attack.

Damn it all. Why was she back here already? With another man capable of hurting her, of sucking her in and pulling the wool over her eyes?

Because it wasn't just the charm, the dancing blue eyes that they had in common now, it was the whole package. The pretending to be one thing and turning out to be another. The hoity-toity status in life and the public-school roots that led to the kind of camaraderie she wanted no more to do with.

Camaraderie that had demoralised her so completely.

A little over a year had passed, and yet if she closed her eyes she could be transported there. Standing at the end of the cramped bar in a London pub, a smile frozen on her face as she'd overheard Adam joking with his old schoolmates, ridiculing her night terrors and the slap he'd taken to his cheek while she'd thrashed about the previous night. They'd all fallen about laughing...until they'd seen her watching them.

She'd run from the pub, refusing to stop until her panic attack had left her no choice. Paralysed on the pavement, unable to breathe, unable to do anything as she'd bowled forward. A kind passerby had taken her in hand, batted away her fiancé when his presence had only made it worse.

She'd returned to the flat that night and he'd been there, remorseful at first, but there was no more fooling to be done. It was over, the truth coming out with it. That he didn't love her any more. That she wasn't fun any more. That he was only sticking it out because he felt sorry for her and the situation with her mother. The *situation…?*

Clutching a hand to her chest, she breathed through the memory. She knew Adam wasn't worth crying over. Knew it. But in that moment with Joel…

Had she been unfair to him? Tainted by her experience with Adam and throwing it all at him?

Possibly. She winced. Most likely.

But then, she'd been blind to Adam's true colours until it was too late. With Joel she could walk away before any real damage was done. He wasn't innocent in what had happened, he'd lied by omission, and by his own confession he wasn't to be trusted around women.

All the warning bells were ringing.

She should keep her distance and be done with it.

Only…he *had* been sweet. A good listener. An understanding one. He couldn't fake all that…could he?

'*I don't think there's anything average about you.*' His words came back to tease her, her heart tripping over them as her body warmed.

Ooh, he was good. And that made him dangerous…regardless of whether he was faking it or not.

She was here to reset her life, carve out a new path, find out what she wanted from it…and that certainly wasn't falling in deep with another man and gifting him the power to hurt her.

But to run away, to avoid the chemistry that fizzed between them whenever they were in the same room, to be the weaker party, just as she'd been weak in front of Adam and his prep boys...

No. She wasn't going there again.

Striding forward, she tugged the bed sheets back and climbed in, her eyes on the ceiling as she made a silent promise to herself. She was going to show him. Show them all.

She wasn't weak. She wasn't running scared. She was going to stick to her plan and be wild. Carefree. Have fun.

And driving Joel to distraction with what he couldn't have—her!—seemed the perfect way to go.

And if anyone wanted to pass judgement, whoopee for them, because she didn't care.

It was time to live for herself. Just as Mum had wanted. Even if tempting the devil wasn't quite what her mother had had in mind.

'Sorry, Mum,' she whispered, 'but you put me on this path and I'm not straying from it.'

Joel Austin would rue the day he'd backed Jessie Rose into a corner. There was no denying that he wanted her—he'd admitted it several times over—and he was so convinced he'd get her. A smile lifted her face...

So, tempt him she would.

CHAPTER SEVEN

Please tell me you're Tokyo-bound...?

JOEL GRIMACED AT the message from his brother and exited it swiftly. Next in his list, his sister:

Call Mum, she misses you. We all do xx

And third, Brendan:

Didn't make it, then...?

He knocked back his mango juice, wishing it were something stronger despite the early hour, his eyes drifting to the glass and the weather beyond. Morning had brought with it more rain and even stronger winds, but the dining room was as tranquil as any oasis. The subtle scent, the gentle music...you could almost forget the storm preventing him from being airborne.

And it wasn't as though he hadn't *tried*. Yes, he'd delayed his departure as long as possible, but there'd still been plenty of time left to fly out. If it hadn't been for that puncture...

He swapped the juice for his phone and opened the message from Brendan. Typed back.

Sorry, bro, we had a blow-out in the Jeep. Lucky to be alive, you know.

Okay, so that was a bit extreme, but he hoped Brendan would see the funny side and go easy on him. No such luck. The phone was ringing before he even had chance to set it down.

He blew out a breath and leaned back in his chair, answering the call.

'Checking I'm in one piece...how kind of you, buddy.'

'Is everyone okay?' Brendan's usually reserved tone was graver still and Joel's grimace made a swift return.

'Hey, chill, we're all good. Though I appreciate the concern.'

Brendan's sigh reached him over the phone. 'You need to learn the art of being subtle, especially in your messages.'

'I'm sure my well-being isn't the true reason you called, so let me put your mind at rest...' For all his arrogance the previous night, courtesy of a few beers, a dented ego and a heightened libido, Jessie had made her feelings pretty clear. He'd be surprised if he caught more than a glimpse of her again if the speed with which she'd fled his company was any indication. And as she'd rightly pointed out, in a house as vast as this, they could quite easily avoid one another.

'Your silence is hardly putting my mind at rest.'

'Give a guy a chance! I was saying Jessie and I are quite comfortable co-habiting until I can get a flight out of here…but if you'd rather I cleared out, I can see if Lady Lottie next door can loan me a bed—I'll risk my body and sleep there.'

Brendan gave a tight chuckle. 'I'm not that desperate to see you gone.'

'So, you do care about my well-being after all?'

'No one deserves that punishment, but I do need to know that Jessie's safe with you around.'

'Seriously, bud?' Now he was offended…not as offended as he'd been last night though.

'She's not like your usual hook-up, Joel. She's delicate, okay—vulnerable and sweet—and I don't want you messing her around.'

'And I already know all of this, so quit with the worrying and—'

Holy Mother of…

He flew forward in his seat, did a double take.

Miss Delicate and Vulnerable and Sweet had appeared in the garden looking—looking… *What* was she wearing? *Doing*, even?

Her auburn hair whipped around her, wild in the wind, dark with the rain. Her sodden white tunic clung to her curves, doing nothing to conceal either skin or underwear. He swallowed. Swallowed again.

What was she *playing* at?

'Joel? *Joel...?*'

'What? Yeah...' He fought to focus on the call. 'What were you saying?'

'What was I saying? You were the one assuring me that you were on best behaviour.'

'Sure, yeah, all of that.'

'Sure, yeah, all of that...what's going on with you? You sound distracted.'

He *was* distracted. Watching as she took in the flowers, the koi, her attention very much on the garden and the pond, and not him. Did she know he was here? Did she know what she *looked* like?

He palmed his face, trying to rub the vision clear, but it was no use, she was still there, like some sinful siren luring him to come out and play...

And play was all he wanted to do.

'Joel!'

'I'm here! Put it down to lack of sleep and too many tequilas and beers at Basil's last night.'

'Basil's. Well, that explains a lot. At least it means you were out of her hair.'

She chose that moment to turn, her eyes clashing with his for the briefest of moments, and then she went back to the garden, the hint of a smile on her lips. Oh, she knew what she was doing all right—his little night nymph was treating him to a daytime view.

Of all the cunning, sneaky...

'You *were* out of her hair, right?' Brendan

dragged him back to the call and he grinned now. Recalling his hands being very much *in* her hair.

'I spent the evening treating Paolo to drinks and food after we spent an eternity hoisting the Jeep out of a ditch and fitting a new tyre.' That was no lie. 'You're welcome, by the way.'

'I'm sure Paolo appreciated the help.'

'Once he got past the whole guest-chipping-in thing. Your staff really need to get over that.'

He sighed. 'And now you're changing the subject.'

'No, I'm tired of it. Tired of you making me out to be some sort of wild playboy with the desire and power to seduce anything in a skirt.'

That earned him a real belly laugh but he wasn't finding it funny.

'You know, she has her own mind, Brendan— she can quite happily reject me if she so chooses.'

'And how often does that happen?'

Not often, if he was honest…but she certainly had last night. Maybe that was why the sight of her wandering through the garden in the turbulent weather was driving him to distraction.

Yeah, yeah, nothing to do with the fact that she's blatantly taunting you.

'She might surprise you.'

'Don't put it to the test.'

'She's a grown adult, Brendan.'

'And she's Hannah's little sister.'

Jessie bent forward, the tunic unveiling the be-ginnings of her luscious… 'She really isn't so little.'

'Joel, don't be a—'

'I've gotta go, bud.' His restraint had snapped, with Brendan, with his nymph. He needed to move. He just wasn't sure where. 'Simone wants me to call Mum and now is the best time. You know how she likes her afternoon nap.'

'You're going to call your mother?' He could hear the doubt mingling with surprise in his friend's voice and he sighed.

'I am.'

He was. *Damn it*, why couldn't he lie? Lying by omission clearly wasn't a problem, but actually lying…especially to Brendan, to whom he owed his life…not possible.

'Well, that's something.'

'Have I ever told you how annoying it is that you have to split your loyalty between my family and me?'

'Your family *is* my family.' There was no jest, no tease. Brendan was stating a fact and it was more sobering than any put-down. 'You guys are all I've got.'

'Always, bro.'

'Now go call Natasha and give her my love.'

'Ciao.'

Joel hung up, his eyes tracking Jessie's movements. Just how long was she planning on staying out there? It was warm enough for sure, but that weather…

His phone buzzed and he glanced at the screen. Simone.

Today would be good, brother. Do I need to remind you what day it is…?

No kisses now and he frowned, realising he
hadn't a clue. Raking a hand through his hair, he
checked the date on his phone and cursed. The
anniversary of Dad's death. His gut rolled, the
blood draining from his face. There was a reason
he didn't keep track of the days…

Taking one last look at Jessie beyond the glass,
her carefree presence giving him the hit of warmth
he'd lost, he dialled his mother and left the room
and the sweet distraction she presented behind.

So maybe going out in the rain and treating him
to the sight he'd given her the night before was a
little obvious, but Jessie appreciated symmetry in
life…and symmetry plus thrilling payback gave
her the advantage.

Or at least it *would* have done if there'd been
any balance in its effect too.

And she wasn't convinced.

She'd met his eye long enough to know that, despite the phone to his ear, his attention had been
very much on her. But had he *wanted* her?

He was gone before she could get a read on
him and as the minutes ticked by and he didn't
reappear or join her outside—*can you blame him
in this weather?*—the buzz gave way to disappointment. And, bitter though it was, she wasn't

backing down. Especially after Hannah's molly-coddling text that morning.

It seemed her sister was already aware of her unexpected house guest and was none too pleased. Whether that was because the guest was a stranger, a man, or because that man was one Joel Austin, she wasn't sure. Going on what Brendan had said via Joel, probably all of the above.

Whatever the case, the message she'd sent along the lines of *Be careful, keep your distance and your wits about you,* felt a little patronising and very OTT. Did Hannah truly think she needed telling? After everything she'd been through with Adam…

When would her sister realise she was perfectly capable of managing her own life? And having a little fun, just as Hannah had ordered, while she was at it…?

She sighed and headed back inside, contemplated going back to her room, drying off and labelling it a bad job, but that stank of giving in. Instead, she headed to the kitchen. She'd grab some juice—not inspired by his sipping his own, honest—and maybe, just maybe happen across him…

She didn't.

Instead, she frightened the life out of poor Margot, who, clutching a hand to her chest, let out a whopping great, 'Good heavens, Miss Rose!'

Brows to the kitchen ceiling, the woman eyed her top to toe, tut-tut-tutting as she took in her damp and bedraggled state. Though not *too* bedraggled. Jessie had purposely applied a touch of waterproof make-up to make sure her eyes were bright, her eyebrows defined, her cheeks a natural-looking pink and lips all glossy.

And all for what? He hadn't even stuck around.

She swallowed the resurging disappointment and smiled. 'Hey, Margot—sorry, I didn't mean to startle you… I came to get some of your lovely juice.' She went to open the fridge but paused, remembering June's reaction the previous day. 'If that's okay with you?'

'Never mind juice, you need to get yourself dry. Shoo. Shoo.' Margot flapped her hands at her. 'You'll catch your death walking through here like that with the air-conditioning blowing like so. I'll bring you your juice!'

She laughed. 'Don't worry, Margot, I'm used to British temperatures and it really is positively balmy in here.'

'I insist, Miss Rose.' Margot was still ushering her towards the door, leaving Jessie no choice but to back up. 'Get yourself changed and I'll bring you juice…and some food—you haven't yet eaten this morning.'

'I'm still stuffed from last night's meal.'

'You and me both…' The voice came from *very* close behind her, and she started. Nervous excitement rushed through her veins, hurried along by something else far more potent.

She turned to face the doorway and the man

now filling it, and was struck by a hot and dizzying sense of *déjà vu*…only this time they had an audience and Joel wasn't just wet, he was…*naked!*

Okay, not quite naked, but did a fluffy white towel slung indecently low on his hips count as being *clothed*?

'Morning,' she burst out, trying not to let her eyes linger on the precarious knot holding the fabric in place. One wrong move and… *OMG.*

She raised her gaze but it only got worse—the triangle of dark hair disappearing south, the thin trail that led up before spreading across pecs that flexed indecently as he used another towel to dry off his very wet hair…

Was he fresh from the shower? Was that where he'd hurried off to…?

Or was this him responding to her provocation in kind?

She met his gaze and read the silent message sparking there: *I see your wet clothing and I raise you a naked body.*

Laughter bubbled up inside, would have come out if she wasn't too busy pressing her lips together to avoid gawping. As for his grin…it was cocky enough already. 'Morning to you too, beautiful.'

Her heart swooned to the floor…*beautiful.*

She hadn't been called that in too long to remember…and when he said it, the *way* he said it, with a delicious hint of gravel-like seduction in his tone…*oh, my!*

'Oh, my…oh, my…' Margot took the words right out of Jessie's mouth but the shudder the older woman gave with them smacked of despair. 'Are you both trying to catch your death? You're making these old bones feel cold! If you both plan on walking around here like this, perhaps we should adjust the temperature.'

Joel chuckled as he continued into the room, gifting her his delicious scent as he passed by, his naked warmth too… He pulled open the fridge and took out the juice. 'No need for that, Margot—I think we're hot enough already.'

He gave Jessie a wink, his eyes dipping over her and projecting the burn…

'You youngsters, I'll never understand you, but I can definitely feed you. I'll bring a spread out to the table shortly if you'd both like to…' her hands were back to flapping '…put some clothes on.'

'Sounds perfect,' Joel said into Jessie's eyes.

'Perfect indeed,' she said into his, disappointment forgotten, challenge accepted. A challenge that made the idea of having to dress sensibly for breakfast too boring for words. Her lips quirked up. 'Though I'm quite happy to dine like this.'

His eyes flashed, his grin stretched to one side as he said again, 'You and me both.'

CHAPTER EIGHT

Eyes concealed by his shades, Joel gave up trying to look busy on his phone and tossed it aside. Stretching out on his sun lounger, he let his gaze drift to where it wanted to go…

Across the way, Jessie was reading a book…the type he'd often seen in his mother's hands. Not that he'd seen her in months, as she'd been swift to remind him when he'd called a couple of days ago, and the memory made his gut clench.

It was by his own choice, of course. His body just hadn't got the memo.

'Stop staring at me.'

She said it without looking up, her sweet, melodic voice doing strange things to his insides… but the strangeness beat the guilt of being an absentee son.

'Can I help it if the view is so appealing?'

Her lips twitched, just enough for him to know she'd clocked his reply. Not enough to indicate whether she appreciated it or not.

They'd been like this for two days. Co-existing. A hint of tease here, a lightly concealed barb there…it was fun.

Though he was fast reaching breaking point

and with no confirmed date for his departure—
the weather was still too turbulent outside of their
sheltered oasis—he was getting perilously close
to breaking his promise to Brendan.

If he had to watch her eat another morsel, her
full lips and appreciative hum working their way
through him hot and fast, or see her stretch out
clothed in nothing more than a bikini at the pool
edge, or worse, watch her push herself up and out
of the pool, water running down every bare inch,
he was going to plead asylum at Lady Lottie's and
be done with it.

Yeah, right, you're never gonna bolt.

His conscience saw his lie for what it was and
he smiled.

'Can I get you a drink?'

She turned to him, her eyes shielded from the
midday sun by the brim of her straw hat, the stunning backdrop of the house that hugged the pool
area protecting them from the elements and fitting her persona so perfectly…and she thought she
didn't belong here. He wanted to shake his head
at her recalled protest.

'Are you trying to put Anton out of a job?'

He shrugged, enjoying the way her eyes dipped
to his exposed chest…yes, he may be hitting the
gym hard every morning to make sure he was in
peak form for her…that and he had to do something to burn off the Jessie-inspired heat. 'Just
keeping myself occupied.'

'You should try reading.'

She went back to her book as though making her point but not before he saw the flush of colour to her cheeks. Question was, what was the cause? Was she hot and bothered because of her attraction to him, or was she hot and bothered because she was frustrated with him...and not in a good way?

He wanted to know.

'Maybe I should...' He rose out of his lounger and approached her—a crazy move probably but he was done resisting the urge. He gestured to the book. 'What are you reading?'

She flicked him a look. 'Are we really doing this?'

'Doing what?' He lowered himself to the lounger beside her.

'Making a conversation about literature?'

He grinned. 'I think you'd prefer discussing that over what I'd like to be doing with my spare time right now.'

Her jaw pulsed. Was she gritting her teeth?

'No, not that, Jessie.'

Her cheeks flushed deeper. 'I wasn't thinking anything.'

'You could have fooled me.'

Because I'm certainly thinking it...

'It's all in your one-track mind, Joel.'

'Really?'

'Yes, really. Now, if you don't mind, I'm getting to a good bit…' She shifted in the lounger, threw her attention into the book.

'If I'm not mistaken,' he couldn't resist saying, 'the good bit in a Mills & Boon isn't too far off what you accused my one-track mind of.'

She pressed her lips together but he got the distinct impression he was close to eking out a laugh.

'What do you know of Mills & Boon?'

'I know my mother likes to read them.'

She raised one brow. Did she think he was making it up to distract her?

'I'm serious. She calls them her one true constant. They never let her down.'

The laugh erupted and she flicked him a look. 'She sounds like a great woman.'

'She is.'

Her eyes narrowed at the sudden sentiment in his voice, sentiment that surprised him too, and he cleared his throat, adding lightly, 'Shame about her offspring though, hey?'

That earned him a smile, a real smile, and he basked in it.

It had taken him two days of this merry and maddening dance. Two days of teasing, eating, fighting, toying…and he'd finally got a smile.

He'd begun to think Jessie was immune to his charm. The more he tried to lure her in, the more she seemed to ignore…no, not ignore…fight back. Never quite coming close enough or holding his eye long enough…but *always* on his radar.

Which only made her appeal more.

Especially when she smiled the way she was smiling now, her laugh soft and teasing as she shook her head. 'How do you do it?'

'Do what?'

'Make people like you?'

He propped his elbows on his knees, his chin in one palm as he studied her. 'I'm not sure *like* is the right word. I've been called annoying, a smart-arse, a prodigy, something of a Lothario…' he wagged his eyebrows, gaining another delightful laugh '…but I'm not sure people actually *like* me.'

Her eyes narrowed…the laughter faded. 'And you're proud of that?'

'I didn't say I was proud.'

'You said it like you are.'

'I said it like I was stating a fact…which I was.'

She frowned. 'And it doesn't bother you?'

Bother him? There were many things that bothered him, like losing his wife far before her time and becoming something of a social pariah, but not being liked…?

'It's each to their own.'

'When it comes to things like taste in food, football teams and the like, sure. But when it comes to being liked by others, don't you think it's ingrained in us to want it?'

'You put that desire first and you'll spend your life bending to the will of others just to win their approval…' *and didn't he know all about that?* '…

who wants to live their life putting other people's needs before their own?'

'People who care about others.'

He shrugged. 'I care… I simply choose to live my life for me now.'

'Now?' She cocked her head to the side. 'So you weren't always this way?'

Trust Jessie to pick up on that tiny detail and what exactly was *'this way'* supposed to mean. Just how did she see him? And why did he care so much about what she thought?

He looked away from her unrelenting gaze, the hairs on his neck prickling under it.

'Joel?'

And, of course, she wasn't going to let him get away without answering.

He studied the waterfall that fed the ponds either side of the pool area, watched the koi beneath the surface, as trapped and contained as he'd once felt.

'I couldn't live my life for me growing up.' His voice sounded as rusty as the memory. 'Like I told you, I was the eldest child, the expectation was that I would follow in my father's footsteps. From very early on, my life was mapped out for me. Get good grades, get my degree, earn the respect of my father's peers and employees so that when the time came I could fill his shoes.'

'That's an awful lot of pressure for anyone to take.'

He dragged his eyes back to hers. 'I didn't know any different. It gave me a drive, a focus, and I met some great people along the way.'

She gave a small smile. 'Like Brendan?'

'Like Brendan...'

Like Katie.

He clenched the edge of his sunbed, fighting off the twist in his gut. When did this conversation get so serious?

'So, what changed?'

He swallowed the bulging boulder in his chest. 'Dad died. I became the CEO and head of the family. Everything was about Austin Industries, and I lived and breathed it. Twenty-four-seven. I lost sight of life outside those office walls, things that should have mattered most passed me by and I hit rock bottom.'

Closing her book, she raised herself to sitting, the three triangles of her leopard-print bikini searing his retinas and proving a welcome distraction to the memories she was dredging up. 'Things? What kind of things?'

'Things that I don't want to talk about.'

'Why?'

'Why does anyone not want to talk about certain things, Jessie?' He regretted the shortness to his voice but he couldn't help it. She had him on edge, pushing him down a path he didn't want to tread.

'I don't know, Joel, but I guess you encouraging me to talk the other day, about Mum and the way my life has gone, helped me come to terms with it a little.'

He gave the smallest of smiles, happy to have at least served some purpose in the brief time they'd known each other...even if it had ended badly.

'I'm glad I could do that for you.'

'But I can't do it for you too?'

The gripe in his gut deepened, his mouth a tight line.

'You'd rather let it fester and grow?'

'It's not—I just—'

Hell, Jessie didn't like him all that much now. How would she feel when she knew the truth? That he'd been so selfish he hadn't even noticed his wife getting sick, hadn't even known she was hiding it from him, carrying the weight of it on her shoulders to protect him and his interests.

No. He couldn't tell anyone. Only Brendan knew the truth—his family had their own versions of it—and even if Jessie forgave him that, the pity that was sure to follow...the compassion he didn't deserve... No. Just no.

'Don't take offence. I don't talk about it to anyone.'

'But maybe it's time you did.'

He couldn't respond, guilt that she had given him her truth and his unwillingness to do the same holding him quiet.

'So now what?' she pressed. 'You've ditched

your responsibilities and you sponge off your mates…is that how this works?'

She gestured to their surroundings, and he gave a low chuckle. 'Not quite. I wasn't lying when I said I have my own wealth and I have people who continue to make it for me. My brothers included…'

Brothers who are doing all the work while you're here in paradise…

Damn it, why did she have to probe?

'But aren't you needed back at base, so to speak?'

'My brothers do okay without me.'

Could she hear the guilt in his voice?

'So, you let your brothers fill your shoes?'

Yes, she could. Of course she could. She didn't miss a thing.

'I guess I do.'

'And you don't miss it?'

'Miss it?'

It wasn't the question he'd expected. In fact, he'd expected her to lay into him, the way he was laying into himself now.

'Yes, the work?'

He'd never stopped to consider whether he missed it, or not.

'I guess there are bits of it I miss. Like the adrenaline buzz when a new project takes off, or a failing one is brought back from the brink, or when a charity event I spearheaded raises a record-breaking sum. But the pressure day in, day out…hell, no.'

'Do you regret walking away?'

No, he didn't regret walking away, because he'd had to. Every second he'd spent in his office, in a suit even, reminded him of how he'd failed Katie. How his obsession to succeed had blinded him to what was going on at home. 'No.'

'Do your brothers not miss you being there?'

Now they were getting to the crux of her questioning, but instead of baulking his mind drifted to Simon and the meeting in Tokyo he would now miss.

'They don't miss my business acumen, they have enough of their own…'

'But they miss you?'

And there it was…

'You got that from my simple statement.'

'I read that in your voice.'

He cleared his throat. 'I see them enough.'

'How often?'

He gave a stilted shrug. 'I don't know.'

'You don't know? What about your mother and your sister?'

'I don't know, Jessie! When did this become an interrogation?'

'When you gave me the impression that you not only walked out on your business but your family too?'

He huffed. 'Hey, steady on, it isn't quite as desperate as all that.'

'Isn't it?'

'I'm taking a break, that's all. An extended break from work and home and having someone to answer to... Is that a crime?'

'I just can't get my head around it. When you have people out there that love you and miss you... you're lucky to have that, and yet you choose to stay away. I have my sister and that's it. There is no one else. Not any more.'

He gripped the edge of the sunbed tighter, his knuckles white as her own loss cut through his armour like a hot knife through butter...twisting deep, searing. He searched for something to say, something that conveyed his sympathy for her situation and excused his own. But what was there to say when the point she made was so brutally accurate and he didn't want to accept it?

He *needed* this time away. He needed it. And she didn't understand because he hadn't told her the full truth.

'It's no surprise you see yourself as unlikeable when you shut out all the people who care about you, Joel. Don't you think you'd be better with them back in your life than to keep running away from them?'

'And why do you care so much?' he threw back, all control lost. 'I'm nothing to you—*hell*, you don't even like me.'

It was fierce, abrupt, but she was pulling him apart—his life, his choices—and he didn't want to examine it. Any of it.

'That might be true.' Blue eyes, bright and steady, held his. 'But perhaps you've misjudged how other people see you…'

He scoffed. 'I don't think so.'

'How do you know?'

'I've had it stated in black and white, Jessie.' Literally. The damning words were all over the internet for anyone to read but he wasn't about to add that. Jessie didn't strike him as a gossip-column fan and he wasn't about to send her looking. 'People can be quite blunt when they want to be.'

'You must have given them good reason.'

'I gave you good enough reason, didn't I?'

She coloured. 'I don't think you did it intentionally.'

'Well, ain't that something…?'

He tried to make it sound light, breezy, as though the slightest softening in her opinion of him didn't matter… They'd go their separate ways soon enough, never to cross paths again, so he didn't *need* to care. Moreover, he'd just *told* her he didn't care for anyone else's opinion, so why wasn't it ringing true?

'Do you turn everything into a joke too?'

He forced a grin. 'Since I changed my life's ambition, absolutely. You ought to try it some time.'

'I don't think so.'

'Why not? You've done your living your life for

others and keeping it all serious, don't you think you've earned your downtime?'

'Downtime, is that what you call it?'

'It's as good a phrase as any. And let's face it, life's far easier to cope with when you only have yourself to worry about.'

Her luscious mouth lifted to one side, her eyes sparking. 'I think you're all mouth and no trousers.'

He eyed his board shorts, cocked a brow. 'Now, that could be arranged…'

Her laugh burst out of her, the sound everything after the darkness that had preceded it. 'And there you go again, making light when *I* think…'

She leaned forward and pressed her finger to his bare chest. The contact had his torso contracting, heat attacking his core as he tried to keep his expression steady, his heart too. He didn't want to hear what was coming, of that he was certain.

'I think you *do* care…you just pretend not to. That way people don't probe beneath the surface and find out what really makes you tick.'

'And I think…' he covered her hand against his chest, flattening her palm to his skin, caught the way her nostrils flared and her lips parted '…you need to throw off your pretty halo and let your hair down.'

Walked right into that one, didn't you, Jessie?

So much for flirting from afar, keeping a safe distance…

Now she couldn't extract her hand, she didn't want to…and as for the suggestion in his eyes… 'How do you propose I do that?'

'Oh, I can think of one or two ways.'

'Are we back to your one-track mind?'

He chuckled, the sound reverberating through her palm, provoking the heat already coursing through her.

'I'll have you know I was thinking more along the lines of physical pursuits—' her brows nudged up '—such as surfing, kayaking, taking a trek out, or driving the Jeep cross-country…generally doing something that doesn't involve having one's nose stuck in a book when the reality around you is far too beautiful to miss.'

She took a shallow breath. 'Last I checked, the weather was still erratic, and the sea looks evil, so I'm not sure *any* of those pursuits are safe right now.'

'Well, in that case, you're forcing me down the safest path…'

'Which is?'

'Back to my one-track mind.'

She gave a tight laugh, her mouth too dry, her head too dizzy, her sister's string of warning texts pleading with her to stay well clear of him bouncing around her mind's eye. And there she'd been, thinking she had it covered…

Hell, maybe she did. Maybe this *was* what she needed. A short-term fling with the promise of nothing more. That knowledge up front gave her the power to keep a lid on it, surely.

And there was no denying that her body craved him.

There was no denying that she cared on some level too.

She wanted to understand what had happened to him after his father's death, what had made him run... He'd said important things had passed him by. But what?

He'd clammed up as soon as she'd pushed but it had to be something huge.

Maybe she should bite the bullet and Google him, but the idea irked her too much and she wouldn't know what was fabricated and what wasn't.

Maybe Hannah would know. And if her sister didn't know, would she be able to find out through Brendan? But asking Hannah would only set her off on one and ruin any reassurance she'd given that she was keeping a safe distance.

As for her private battle, their little game...

'So, you admit you have a one-track mind?' she whispered, wetting her lips.

'I admit nothing.'

His eyes dipped to her mouth, their darkened depths injecting her with dopamine just as his arrogant promise from two days prior permeated the lustful haze: *'I very much intend for you to kiss me first.'*

And you will if you don't break this connection, right now.

Had that been his plan all along? To play the tortured soul and get her to cave first? Of all the… She snapped her hand back and shot to her feet, book clutched to her chest. 'Oh, no, you don't.'

He frowned up at her. 'Huh?'

'Very clever, Joel.' She shook her head to clear away the lustful dregs and stepped away. 'Playing the tormented card to get me to feel sorry for you and then moving in for the kill…'

'Moving in for the…?' He rose to his feet, his frown deepening. 'What are you talking about?'

'Oh, like you don't know,' she threw back, hurt that she could be so foolish, so stupid, so gullible. Joel wasn't wounded. He wanted to win. She gripped her hat to her head as a gust of wind threatened to take it away, and glared at him. '*"I very much intend for you to kiss me first."* Ring a bell?'

His eyes widened. 'You're not serious? That was a cocky statement born of a cocky hour. I said it on impulse. I didn't mean…'

'Impulse, hey? And how many other things have you said on impulse to get a woman into bed?'

'Jessie, come on…' He went to step towards her, but she got to him first, her finger back on his chest, and this time it was all anger firing through her bloodstream. Anger at him, at Adam, at life for taking away her mother…

'Don't you *come on* me, I wasn't born—'

Another gust of wind sent her unrestrained hat flying and she threw her hand out to grab it but Joel was quicker…quicker but unsteady on his feet. One minute he was standing, the next he was airborne. He hit the pool with a resounding belly flop, showering her in water and disappearing beneath its surface.

'Oh, God!' She tossed the book aside and dropped to her knees, gripping the pool edge as she leaned over. What if he'd hit his head going in? Belly flops alone could hurt, right? Could they render you unconscious too? Was she going to have to rescue him?

His body emerged with force, his choked splutter the most amazing sound to her panicked pulse. 'Are you okay?'

He threw his head back, swiped the water from his eyes as he grasped at her hat bobbing innocently away.

'I'm fine…' his cheeks blazed, his grimace a sight '…my pride not so much.'

He was embarrassed. Joel. Embarrassed? She bit back a laugh—he had, after all, hit the deck trying to rescue her hat.

'Are you laughing at me?' Blue eyes clashed with blue, the challenge in his depths unmissable.

'No.'

'You are, you're laughing!'

'Well, you've got to admit, it is a little funny…'

'You find my humiliation amusing?'

She couldn't contain her grin now. 'I'm sure your pride can take it.'

'And what about yours?'

'My—' before she could work out what he was about, his hand was around her wrist, one sharp tug and… 'Joel!'

She fell into the water with a squeal, clamped her mouth shut as she went under, her brain a furious chant—

Of all the annoying, childish, pathetic…

She kicked to the surface, her own cheeks bright. 'How dare you?' she spluttered, scraping her hair out of her face as she furiously trod water.

'You started it.' He backed away, one palm out as if he was trying to swear his innocence, his eyes alive with tease. 'You've got to admit, though, you needed cooling down.'

'*I* needed cooling down.'

'Yup.' He placed her hat on his head and continued backing up as she came after him. 'Your pride, to be precise.'

'*My* pride?' she choked on a laugh—and a mouthful of water. *Elegant. So elegant.* 'You are un-freaking-believable.'

'And yet I rescued your delightful hat…'

He gestured to said hat, which suited him in a strange kind of a way, and the sudden proprietorial spark over Joel of all people had her snatching her hand out.

'A hat I would appreciate back.'

He evaded her reach. 'You would?'

She kicked after him but he made swimming backwards look effortless. 'You don't seem to want it that badly…'

'Well, if you'd just stop…'

'And spoil the fun…'

The tickling sensation in her belly grew with the exertion. She felt like a child playing chase. It was ridiculous. And fun. And he had her laughing all over again. Didn't matter what warnings her heart and brain wanted to deliver. She liked him. And she was having more fun than she'd had in years. 'How old are you?'

'Thirty-five. I'm not sure why that's relevant.'

'I bet you were a nightmare with the girls at school. Stealing their possessions to get their attention…'

'Is that what you think I'm doing?'

'I *know* that's what you are doing…' And it felt good. *Seriously* good. She couldn't stop laughing as he chuckled with her.

His back came up against the edge of the pool, trapping himself into a corner, and she made a triumphant leap for the hat before realising her mistake. Ducking her arm, he swam around her, and she turned too. Her back was against the wall, her front facing his only a few feet away.

The predator had become the prey…

'At least I've got you laughing with me rather than at me now,' he said as he came towards her.

'So I am…' It was breathless. Giggles, exertion, excitement and everything in between. She gripped the side with one hand, lifted the other. 'Hat?'

'Say please?'

'Please,' she chuckled.

He closed in on her, the banked desire in his eyes making her breath hitch. 'What about a pretty please?'

'Don't push your luck.'

'How about an agreement to be friends again?'

The sudden glint of seriousness in his eye tugged at her heartstrings and silenced the laugh she would have given. Instead, she gave a brusque nod. 'Friends.'

His mouth lifted to one side, the glint evaporating into a sparkle of tease. 'Friends with…'

He wagged his eyebrows and just like that she was laughing again.

She snatched the hat back with a shake of her head. 'Again, don't push your luck!'

She turned and pressed herself up and out of the water, knowing full well that if they stayed any longer the appeal of his mostly naked body and her sorely neglected libido would see to it that he got exactly what he hinted at, and then where would she be…?

Having some wicked fun, that's where!

She slowed her exit from the pool, gave him an extended view of her wet bikini-clad behind and swore she heard him groan, her body warming in tune.

Was she crazy to turn down the opportunity of a lifetime—sex with someone who only had to do so much as look at her and she was turned on—while on the holiday of a lifetime?

She'd never stay anywhere like this again...

She'd likely never meet another man who made her feel like this again...

She didn't know what the future held but she did know she'd regret it if she let him slip through her fingers without experiencing all that he was offering.

So long as she kept in mind what this was. No strings. No future. No pain.

'Joel...?' It came out softly as she turned, her eyes locking with his.

He tilted his head to the side, his eyes narrowing. 'Yes.'

'Life is the adventure you make it, Jessie—live it, love it, no regrets.'

She breathed through her mother's words.

Far be it from me to fight with you, Mum...

CHAPTER NINE

OKAY, WHAT HAD he missed?

Because one minute he was looking at one amazing behind and envying every rivulet of water that ran down Jessie's lightly freckled thighs, knowing she was leaving and that he'd been parked firmly in the friend zone, and the next…

She was lowering herself to sit at the pool edge, her bottom lip caught in her teeth and a thousand X-rated wants in her eyes…or at least that was what he thought he was seeing.

'You know that suggestion you made…?'

'Which one?' he asked carefully, his pulse upping a notch.

'Well, there was the suggestion that I should enjoy more active pursuits, and then there was the other…'

Cheeks reddening, her voice trailed off and he stepped towards her. 'The other?'

'The friends thing…' She swirled her legs in the water as though she couldn't sit still.

'What about it?'

He paused before her, reaching out to rest his palms on the smooth stone either side of her thighs, the heat from her skin making his own buzz. Her feet brushed against his board shorts and he clenched his jaw. He wouldn't be getting out of this pool any time soon...but with any luck she'd come back in and join him.

'The way I see it we have a couple of nights together if the weather forecast is correct, and you're right, I should spend more time appreciating the view...'

He nodded, her feet persisting with their teasing caress, her eyes—her eyes were eating him alive...or was that a figment of his overactive and hopeful imagination?

'And that view...it includes you.'

No, not imagining it at all...

His mouth tilted up at the corner. 'I'm glad you like what you see.'

'Don't be getting cocky, now.'

'Moi...?' He would have grinned full-on if he wasn't fighting to keep his cool. 'I wouldn't dare.'

She chuckled softly, one hand reaching out to stroke his hair from his face, the move so gentle and surprising that his pulse skittered, his breath snagged.

'Good, because I'm tempted by the benefits too.'

'The friends *with* benefits?' Was she truly serious?

She hummed. 'There's only one problem...'

'Which is?'

'I swore I wouldn't kiss you first.'

So that was what this was about, his cocky promise again… 'You did.'

'And you swore I would.'

'I did.' *Idiot.*

'So, you see, it's a bit of a problem for me…'

'A problem you'd like me to fix?'

She gave him a coy smile, her eyes giving him an evocative look that he was rapidly losing himself to…

'I'm open to ideas.'

Instinct taking over, he cupped her calves, pulling her legs apart so he could step between them. '*Now* you're open to ideas.'

Her eyes flashed and his body pulsed. She wasn't stopping him and slowly, ever so slowly, he lowered his mouth to the inside of her thigh, just above the knee…he grazed her skin with his lips, the tip of his tongue, caught her sharp intake of breath, the way her hands shot to the pool edge to steady herself.

'These kisses don't count, right?'

'No…' she rasped out. 'No, they don't count.'

'Or these?'

He moved along her thigh, her body trembling and tensing the higher his caress reached, the smallest of squeaks escaping her lips as he stopped just short of her briefs.

'Okay?' he murmured, teasing the soft flesh with his tongue.

'More than,' she gently huffed, the need in her eyes, the flush to her skin tugging at his aching groin.

This was more fun than he'd had in years. And he'd *had* fun. This—*she*—was something else. He rose up, his chest brushing along her torso, her breasts, until they were mouth to mouth and he didn't care any more. To hell with the wager. To hell with losing…

He combed his fingers through her hair, inhaled her sweet scent and kissed her. Kissed her as if she was his for the taking. As if she was food, water, air, and everything his body needed. Everything he craved. Kissed her and acknowledged that if this was how losing felt, he'd lose a hundred times over and still come back for more.

She whimpered into his mouth, her legs wrapping around him, squeezing him closer and he was losing his mind, his control, where he was…and he couldn't afford to. They were outside. The staff were somewhere. If Brendan learned of this…

'Damn Brendan!' he groaned, tearing his mouth away.

She flung herself back, eyes darting, head turning. 'Brendan! What? Where?'

'No, no…' He cupped her face, stroked her cheeks with his thumbs, cursing the interruption as the ache within him built. 'He's not here, just in my head.'

'While we were kissing?' She winced. *'Really?'*

His chuckle was tight. 'I'm aware that his spies are very much everywhere.'

'You mean the staff.'

He nodded. 'And he'll make sure Anton has my head if he learns of this.'

She frowned at him, her eyes bemused. 'Why? You're a guest of his. I'm a guest of his...'

'And, like I already told you, by association to Hannah you are very much off-limits.'

She tilted her head to the side, hooked her hands around his neck. 'I thought you liked living a little dangerously.'

She's got you there.

'There's living dangerously, and then there's being something of an exhibitionist, and the things I want to do to you, with you, I'd rather do in private.'

She choked on a laugh, her cheeks flushing deeper. 'My room, then?'

'I feared you'd never ask.'

He scanned the deserted poolside, the rooms through the expanse of glass. Hell, they'd most likely already been seen, and Brendan would be issuing him with an eviction notice come morning, but for now...

'You go, I'll follow.'

You're really going to do this? his conscience pricked, his promise to Brendan weighing heavy on his shoulders.

But as she rose up, her body glistening in the

sun, a smile to die for on her lips, his brain emptied out and his body took over.

'Don't be long,' she murmured.

'Oh, I won't.'

She dipped to grab her book and the hat that he'd knocked free, and with a seductive sway of the hips she disappeared inside, leaving him at war with himself.

And Brendan.

He didn't want to actively go against his friend's wishes but then, his friend wasn't here. His friend hadn't seen the temptation first-hand and the mutual promise of keeping it simple. No broken hearts. No trouble. Just two days or so of fun.

And he could provide her with that and more.

Mind tripping over itself with the many and varied options at their disposal, he got out of the pool, grabbed his phone from the side table and left his nagging conscience behind.

'Wow, your room is so...orderly.'

'Isn't yours?' The staff were like fairies, sweeping through the many rooms unseen, keeping everything clean and shiny.

'Not like this...'

She looked around her, seeing it how he must. Everything had its place, her hair and make-up all lined up in order of size, her books beside the bed in a neat pile sorted by colour, her phone, watch and bracelet from Mum that she avoided wearing by the pool all symmetrically set out on her bedside table.

She scrunched up her nose. 'I will admit I have a touch of OCD about me.'

He placed his phone next to hers, his brows lifting. 'A touch?'

'Hey.' She nudged him. 'Carry on with that attitude and you can go back the way you came.'

'I'm not judging.'

'Of course you're not.'

In one swift move he tugged her up against his chest, his lips claiming hers and stealing what breath she had left.

'I'll have you know,' he broke away enough to say, 'there's nothing I don't love about you.'

His eyes were hooded, his lips grazing against hers as he seemed to swear it as an oath, and heaven help her, she was overwhelmed, his declaration making her heart pound, her head swim. Didn't matter if he'd said it off the cuff, it felt like more, teasing her with the impossible, and that scared her, her sanity pleading with her to back up a step…

Don't get swept up in him. He's not the man to get swept up in. This will be over as quickly as it has begun.

'We'll see,' she said, projecting a confidence she didn't quite feel. 'Give it another day or two and you'll have tired of my anal ways.'

'Anal, you say…'

'Oh, God…' She covered her face. 'You're incorrigible!'

He snatched her hands away. 'You were the one that suggested—'

'Joel!' She went to shove him and he grabbed her up in the air, trapping her squeal with his kiss as he rolled her back onto the bed, his hot, hard body covering her top to toe, one arm planted in the bed to avoid crushing her so completely. Though being crushed by him felt like a super-fine way to go.

'What am I going to do with you?' she murmured, and he chuckled low in his throat, traced kisses along her jaw as he stroked one hand down her side.

'I can think of plenty of things…'

A thrilling shiver ran through her. 'I bet you can.'

He'd know all the tricks, have all the experience, and there she was, celibate for over a year and hardly that adventurous before then…if Adam was to be believed.

He dipped to the edge of her bikini top and she bit her lip, her hands stilling in his hair as sudden panic set in.

'Before you go any further,' she rushed out, 'I need to tell you something.'

'Fire away, baby, but if this is about me getting tired of you…' He caressed the curve of her breast with his chin, his stubble providing enough friction to send her toes curling into the mattress.

'No. Well, not quite. I just…' She chewed the

inside of her cheek, trying to find the courage to admit it.

'If this is about protection, I have…'

She shook her head. 'No—No. It's not about that.' And why was she blushing when condoms were a sensible and important and grown-up thing to discuss? 'I just haven't done this in a while.'

His eyes lifted, his gaze softening as he rose up over her, stroked her hair back from her face… Lord, his eyes were so blue…so thrillingly, illicitly, drown-yourself-in-them blue. All the more with the compassion shining there. Why, oh, why was he so wrong for her again?

'If it makes you feel any better, I haven't either.'

She gave a choked laugh, desire and disbelief trapping it inside. 'Yeah, right, pull the other one.'

'You don't believe me?' His brows drew together and she shifted beneath him, guilt gnawing at her even though he had to be joking. Surely. He'd even told her his reputation wasn't great when it came to women—what else could he have meant?

'From what I've learned…it seems unlikely.'

'Are we back to you making assumptions about me?'

She coloured, the discomfort growing. 'I—'

'Or have you been reading up on me?'

'What?' It was her turn to frown. 'No…everything I've learned, I've learned from you. I haven't *read* a thing.'

He gave a soft laugh, bowed his head and shook it. 'You're something else.'

Anger spiked in her blood. 'What the hell is that supposed to mean?'

The last person to say that to her had been Adam…granted, his tone had been far more derisive, but still it was a timely reminder to protect herself, to keep her walls in place.

'Jessie—'

She shook her head, pressing him away as she rolled out of bed.

'I'm sorry…' He scrambled after her. 'I didn't mean it in a bad way.'

Rounding on him, she put her hands on her hips and he stopped, his knees planting into the mattress.

'How else could you mean it?'

'Hell, if you knew what I'm used to…' He scraped his hair out of his eyes, pinned her with his gaze. 'No one meets me without knowing me and realising you didn't was a breath of fresh air. The idea that you still haven't been tempted to look me up is…well, it's unreal.'

'And yet it's the truth, so get over yourself!'

'Hey, don't be mad, please, Jessie. You don't understand. People who meet me, they know everything about me before we've even said one word. Or at least they *think* they know everything about me.'

'Because people talk?'

'Because the press and people talk.'

'You really think you're that interesting?'

'They seem to think so.' His mouth quirked. 'You don't get to be an Austin heir without being the talk of the press.'

'Yeah, well, I'd rather get my facts from the horse's mouth.'

He gave an edgy laugh. 'Does that make me the horse?'

'I guess it does.'

Though she wasn't smiling, she wasn't anything. She felt stupid. Dumb.

Millions if not billions of people would know all about him, his demons included, truth or not, why hadn't she just got on and Googled him?

He reached for her and she let him take hold, her body craving the reassuring heat of his even though she likely shouldn't.

'I *love* that you haven't chosen to take anyone else's word over mine.' He wrapped his arms around her. 'Please believe me.'

She pressed away from his chest to look up into his eyes. 'Then why do I feel like some naïve idiot?'

'You're no idiot.' His eyes flashed back at her. 'You're special and you're different. In all the right ways.'

'You sure about that?'

'I've never been surer about anything. I *love* that you're taking me at face value, that for all your prejudice—which does suck, by the way, and I'm determined to prove you wrong—it hasn't come from the gossip columns. You haven't chosen to believe them over the man before you...'

She pursed her lips. 'It's just come from me and my hackneyed idea of the men that come from your world—like that sounds so much better!'

'It works for me...' He dragged a soft kiss over her lips, dipped to kiss her jaw, her throat, her chest...

'Well, it doesn't for me and I'm sorry!' she puffed out, resting her palms on his shoulders as she arched back, giving him greater access though keeping her distance too because she wasn't ready to let go just yet...not if she could learn more of the truth from the horse himself. 'But give me a moment and I can Google you and get up to speed if you like?'

She stepped away, reinforcing her point, and he tugged her back. 'Oh, no, you don't.'

'I'll make you a deal, then.' She softened against him, hooking her hands around his neck. 'I won't Google you if you tell me the truth—is this why you didn't tell me who you were when we met?'

His eyes raked over her face, the torment in their blue depths too deep to mean nothing—what wasn't he saying?

'Please, Joel,' she pressed softly. 'If we're going to do this, I deserve to understand why you didn't tell me.'

'You have no idea what it's like, Jessie, to live a life where it's not just your parents you have to prove yourself to, it's the world too. Everyone's waiting for you to fail, make a mistake, to prove you're not worth the money you were born into… either that, or they're hoping to wed you and run away with your money.'

She breathed in his reasoning. 'You liked that I saw you as someone normal, someone like me, no expectations, no nothing?'

'Yes, is that so wrong?'

'Not when you put it like that.'

But his eyes remained haunted. Did it really cut as deep as that? She understood the pressure of responsibility, but he looked utterly broken by it.

Was it his father? Dealing with his grief and the pressure of stepping into his father's role simultaneously, the press attention exacerbating it all? No freedom to grieve, no space to look weak and just be?

She reached out, cupped his face. 'Well, Joel Austin, I couldn't care less whether you are a billionaire or a pauper, this connection between us is real and I want to explore it, exploit it, and have the holiday of a lifetime with you in it.'

And then she kissed him, kissed him until he was all fire, no ice, and it was all about the present, not the past or the future.

Just pleasure.

CHAPTER TEN

JOEL STARED AT his face in the mirror and hated himself.

Hated himself for losing himself so completely in the passion Jessie had stirred up, a passion so intense he'd only ever felt it with one other person.

Katie.

The only woman he had ever loved. The only woman he would ever love—or so he'd thought.

He'd sworn that would be it. He'd never be that vulnerable again.

But Jessie had dug beneath his skin, got him to talk more than he had in years, and still he hadn't told her the full truth, holding back that part of him in the hope that he could keep his distance. Prevent a bond building, a bond that neither of them wanted. A bond that was reserved for Katie.

But not telling her about Katie felt like a betrayal in itself. To Katie's memory and Jessie's good heart.

He hadn't lied when he'd said Jessie was special. God, no.

And there *was* something between them. Something strong and undeniable.

Her loving nature and loyal bond to her family,

her sensitive and honest demeanour…she was similar to Katie in so many ways, but Katie had been born into his world. She'd been accustomed to it. She hadn't come after him for his money or his status. They'd met at university, become friends then lovers, and finally the golden couple in the eyes of the press. Loved-up and happy with it.

And he hadn't minded those articles. Lauded for being in love, criticised for being distracted by it too, because he had been.

It was the ones that had come later. After his father's death and he'd thrown himself into work, when news of her possible illness had hit the headlines and he'd been away on yet another business trip. Seeing the photo they had captured, having his eyes opened to it…

Flying home early to confront her and seeing the answer in her hollow cheeks, her shadowed eyes, before she'd even told him…and he should have known. He should have been the first to question. Not some stranger of a journalist focused on his next major scoop.

He gripped the edge of the sink, swallowed the rising bile. He couldn't tell her about Katie because he couldn't admit how he'd failed the woman he had loved with his all.

'Hey…'

He spun on the spot to find Jessie in the doorway, a bedsheet wrapped around her, a tentative smile on her lips. She'd never looked more vulnerable, more sweet…more different from himself.

'Hey.' It was a croak and she cocked her head, her perceptive antennae clearly buzzing.

'You okay?'

He raked an unsteady hand through his hair, tried to smile. 'Of course, how could I not be?'

Her brows drew together. 'You've been gone a while…'

'I have.'

'Uh-huh.' She stepped inside, the crease between her brows deepening. 'You don't seem okay…are you sure there's nothing wrong?'

He reached out, craving the comfort she seemed to effortlessly bring, and she stepped into his embrace, pressed her warm, soothing body up against his. He inhaled her sun-kissed scent—jasmine, vanilla, coconut—breathed it out slowly. 'Have you always been this perceptive?'

'Hardly. But after what we shared I wasn't expecting you to high-tail it out of bed so quickly… Did I do something wrong?'

And there was the sensitivity, the vulnerability…

'No. God, no.' He pressed her away to look down into her eyes, guilt pinching at his heart. 'Why would you think that?'

'I don't know…' she wet her lips '…you're the one hiding out in the bathroom. I'm a little out of practice but usually there's something of a snuggle afterwards or at least a goodbye of sorts.'

'A snuggle?'

She nudged him. 'You know what I mean.'

'I do. And frankly, that sounds like a great idea, but...' He kissed her forehead, took another breath for courage '...there's something I need to tell you and for that I need a drink.'

He felt the tension ripple through her. 'So, there is something wrong?'

'Not with you, baby,' he admitted softly.

'But...?'

'Come on...' he encouraged her back into the bedroom and dipped to lift his swimming trunks from the floor, tugging them on. 'I'll be back soon. I'm just going to change into some dry clothes and get that drink. You want one?'

'Please. Whatever you're having is fine.'

The hesitation in her eyes almost had him staying, taking back his words, but he couldn't. He had to do this. For her. For him. For Katie.

He was back within minutes, clothed in a white T-shirt and shorts, two glasses of rum in hand. The glass doors were open and she was wrapped in a soft pink robe, looking out over her private garden, the infinity pool lapping gently at her feet. The sky had grown heavy, the ocean rolling wild in the distance, the palms taking a beating by the wind, but he got the impression she wasn't seeing any of it.

'I hope rum's okay?' he said, more to announce his presence.

She turned, her smile faint. She eyed the drink he offered out, tightened her robe before taking it. 'Neat?'

'The local way, baby,' though his cheeky tease was doused by the mood as heavy as the sky above.

'Look…' She dragged in a breath, lifted her gaze to his. 'If you're about to tell me you have a girlfriend, or—or a wife—I'd appreciate you—'

'Whoa, Jessie!' The mention of a wife had more power than she could know, and it shuddered right through him. 'Do you really think I'd let things go this far if I had a woman somewhere?'

Her throat bobbed, her eyes flashing with some unknown emotion. 'So, you're single?'

'Yes!'

She blew out a breath. 'Thank heaven.'

'I'm so glad you're relieved.' Though he wasn't… for all that they'd shared, she still thought him capable of an affair, adultery even.

'When you said you had more to tell me and you looked so—so tormented, I thought the worst.'

'The worst of me, you mean?'

'I'm sorry.' She touched his arm, her eyes glistening with her apology, and he shook his head, looked off into the distance to avoid her eye and the way she was making him feel.

'Don't be.' He threw back his rum and she palmed his chest, called his eyes back to her.

'I am. I'm sorry. I'm afraid I'm prone to thinking the worst.'

He searched her gaze. 'Your fiancé?'

'Him. Me. My anxiety. Life. It likes to throw us curve balls all the time.'

He stared into her eyes a moment longer, wishing he could take away their sadness, but instead he knew he was about to add to it.

'What is it, Joel? Please, just tell me?'

He covered her palm on his chest, felt the words stick in his throat.

'You can tell me anything...' she whispered.

'I know.' It was barely audible, the pressure in his chest suffocating. He couldn't be this close to her and let it out. He needed room. Space without her touch. Air without her scent.

'It's okay, Joel.'

'No—no, it's not okay.' He shook his head, stepped away. It would never be okay again. And talking of it only made it real again. He looked to the horizon and stopped thinking, stopped feeling, just spoke...

'I don't ever talk about it, about her...'

He sensed her tension. 'Her?'

'Katie.' He flicked her a look. 'My wife.'

Her eyes widened, her lips parting with her sudden breath. 'You said you weren't married...'

'I'm not.' His voice dulled with the pain of his

confession, his acceptance, his eyes dragging back to the view. 'Not any more.'

'You're d-divorced?'

'Widowed.'

She gasped, stepped towards him, but something about his stillness must have stopped her. 'I'm so sorry.'

He barely heard her. His mind was already on the past, on the early days when he'd first met Katie and life had been incredible. He rarely let the memories in, but he did now...relived them... let their bittersweet warmth fuel the words that left his lips.

'I didn't believe in soulmates, love at first sight, any of that crazy stuff...but the second I saw her, I knew...'

Jessie shifted in the periphery of his vision, her hand rising to her mouth, her heart breaking for him...he could tell. And if he looked in her eyes now he'd see the pity...the pity he didn't deserve.

'We were inseparable, as inseparable as we could be with our work and social commitments. She was the face of a charity, and I had my father and a multi-billion-dollar company to prove myself to, but we made it work. We were...happy.'

He forced back more rum, needing the heat to contend with the chilling shift inside, as dark and tormented as the memory of what came next.

'When my father died and the pressure increased tenfold, I had to be away more and she couldn't always be there. She stopped wanting to travel so much, claimed it tired her out and she wanted to be at home to focus on the progress she was making with the charity, on making a future home for our children too...' His voice cracked but he forged ahead. 'I should have realised she was sick. I should have seen what was going on, but I was too preoccupied with the business...'

'Your grief too—you'd just lost your father—'

'I was her husband! I should have known!' he spat out, making her flinch, and he pressed his fist to his forehead. 'I'm sorry...'

She shook her head softly, her eyes damp at the corners. 'You have every right to be angry, but not at yourself...'

'Of course at myself. I should have noticed the weight loss. I should have noticed how tired she was. How she flinched when she stood. How she couldn't eat the foods that she'd once loved. How I'd pour a glass of her favourite wine and she'd only drink half at most.'

'But you did notice—'

'I noticed when it was too late. I noticed when a press article was pushed in my face and the question was there in black and white. *What is wrong with Katie Austin?* Can you believe it? I was thousands of miles away and some stranger had snapped a picture that portrayed more than my own eyes had seen in the flesh.'

'Maybe you knew deep down, and you didn't want to see it?'

He scoffed. 'Do you think I'm that heartless?'

'No. But when my mother first came out of the hospital, I didn't want to see the signs. I didn't want to acknowledge that the accident was just the beginning of a steady deterioration that would one day take her from me.' Her voice vibrated with her own pain, her own agony. 'Is it not possible that you didn't want to see it?'

He choked on a laugh. 'Do you think I would have let her go through it alone out of some selfish need to protect *myself*?'

'No, that's not what I'm saying. But we're only human and sometimes when we can't control something so—' her throat bobbed '—so final, self-preservation forces us to block it out it.'

Was she right? On some level, is that what he'd done? No, he couldn't believe it, only…

'How did you find out? I don't mean the news report, I mean for real, the truth…'

'She told me eventually…when I confronted her with the article in hand.'

'How long had she known?'

He stared at her, not wanting to admit it but feeling the words leave his lips anyway. Distant. Detached. 'A month. She'd known and kept it to herself for a month.'

She stepped towards him slowly. 'A month

where I imagine she was coming to terms with it herself.'

'A month where I should have been by her side, fighting the damn thing!'

She touched a hand to his cheek, looked deep into his eyes. 'My mother never wanted to be treated like she was ill. She didn't want to be mollycoddled or suffocated by nurses, or by me, or my sister. Most of the time, we pretended it didn't exist. She'd have a seizure, we'd deal with her relapse, and we'd go again. She'd lose the strength, the mobility, and I'd do what I could to help her recover. But we'd never focus on the end, and your wife, your Katie, she wouldn't have wanted you to do that either.'

'But a month, Jessie, a *whole month* where she wrestled with the realisation. She took the decision to do nothing. Nothing! They said they could buy her a year, maybe more, and she said no. No! I wasn't worth that. The time we could have had, time together that—that—' He shook his head, pain swallowing up his words.

'She would have had her reasons.'

'Reasons I don't understand. And I know it sounds selfish. It was her life. But it was my life too! We made a promise, in sickness and in health, until death do us part…' He shook his head again, squeezed his eyes shut against the pain. 'She broke that vow.'

'No, she didn't. She loved you and she wanted to protect you and the time you had left.'

'But I wasn't there when she needed me most and I begged her, pleaded with her to do something, anything.'

'But nothing could change the inevitable, Joel.'

His body juddered with a sob so raw and unrestrained that for the first time he truly let it in. His hurt, his pain, his shame, the betrayal that he'd lain at Katie's door without truly acknowledging it before.

The glass slipped from his grasp until he realised it was Jessie taking it away, placing it on the side before she came back to him.

'It's okay, Joel.' She pulled him in, her body warm, her voice softly soothing as she wrapped her arms around him. 'It's okay.'

'But it's not, it's not...she's gone... I'll always love her...and she's gone...'

Her hand was in his hair as he buried his face in her shoulder, her fingers gently stroking as he let the tears fall—hot, angry, long overdue.

'I should have been there for her, Jessie. I should have pushed work aside and just been there for her. I should never have lost sight of what mattered most.'

'And you *were* there for her. When she truly needed it, you *were* there. And yes, you may have argued with her, pleaded with her, and all she would have heard was your love for her and your pain.'

He couldn't stop shaking his head but inside her words were resonating, taking hold, shining a new light on a dark truth that he'd trapped inside for so long.

'Is this why you've run from your life, Joel? Why you won't go back home?'

He took an unsteady breath, lifted his head to see her own cheeks damp, her eyes bright with understanding and drawing out the rest of his sorry tale.

'After she died, I lost myself. I was so angry, I lashed out. My family, Brendan... I treated them all so badly. I started drinking too much, taking painkillers, anything to numb the pain. If it weren't for Brendan...' he swallowed, remembering that one fateful night...the bits he'd been lucid enough to remember '... I wouldn't be here now.'

Her brows twitched, her words a whisper. 'I'm sure that's not—'

'No, Jessie, it's true. I wouldn't. He found me out cold one night and got me to the hospital. If he hadn't—if he'd been only a few minutes later... I owe him my life. No one knows. Not my family. Only Brendan.'

'Oh, Joel...' Fresh tears rolled down her cheeks, her palms trembling as she cupped his face. 'I'm sorry, I'm so sorry, but you must know that your family love you. It doesn't matter what you think you've done. What wrongs you believe you've committed. They love you.'

He did know that deep down and yet…

'You can't outrun your past, sweetheart.'

Sweetheart. The way she said it… His mind travelled back to a different time, a different woman, his heart beating back to life against his will, the warmth creeping in…

'You can only take control of your future. Don't you think you owe it to Katie, to your father too, to return home, to live it alongside your family who love you and must now be grieving their loss of you too?'

He stepped out of her reach, dragged a hand down his face and stared at the world rather than her. He took an unsteady breath, and another, but it wasn't enough to strip the memory of their faces. 'I can't stand it, Jessie. The look in their eyes, the pity, the compassion…'

'Because you feel you don't deserve it. But you do. You need to forgive yourself and move forward before life passes you by and the time you have left with those you love is gone.' He dared to look at her, taking in the grief etched in her face as she said quietly, 'I only have my sister left, Joel. You have an entire family that cares about you, Brendan too…don't lose sight of that.'

And she cared about him.

Jessie didn't say it out loud, she didn't need to.

She was sure Joel could read it in her face, and she wasn't going to run from it. Right now, the risk to her heart mattered far less than the anguish Joel had yet to come to terms with.

'And I know part of me is being a hypocrite,' she admitted, 'because I'm judging you for running from your life when I do exactly the same every time I pick up a book.'

He scoffed, his lips quirking. 'I hardly think that's one and the same.'

'No?' She raised her brows, challenging him. 'Books are my safety blanket to hide under. When life's getting too much and I need to run from the real world, I read. When my anxiety attacks start to become more frequent, I read more and more…'

He cocked his head. 'Have you always suffered with anxiety?'

'When I was younger but I grew out of it. Mum's accident brought it all back. I don't know whether it was the realisation that we can't control everything that happens to us, that one day things can be fine and the next…' She pressed her palm to her chest, breathed through the building noise within. 'She was popping to the shops, that was all, wrong place, wrong time when the driver lost control on black ice. It could have happened to anyone.'

'I'm sorry, Jessie.'

'I know.' Her smile was rueful. 'Afterwards, I just felt helpless. The only thing I could do was be there for her. Help her when she needed it, look after her, but I couldn't change what had happened. I couldn't stop the seizures. I couldn't prevent the inevitable. And then I started to see danger everywhere—a trip to the shops, a walk in the park, *any* outing became another bad incident waiting to happen. I stopped watching the news, listening to the radio…became a homebody.'

'I guess I can understand that.'

'It's why my sister sent me here, hoping I'd get something of life, a bit of adventure…'

'Instead you get lumbered with me?'

She laughed softly, happy to have the subtle spark of teasing back in his eyes. 'Oh, I don't know, I think you've turned out to be a key part of that experience.'

'Is that so?'

She nodded, her chest easing as she closed the distance he had created. 'So, how about we make each other a promise?'

'A promise?'

'A pact of sorts?'

'I'm listening…'

'I'll put down the books and throw myself into those other pursuits you mentioned…'

His brows lifted. 'Pursuits?'

'Like the surfing, the all-terrain driving…all things you could teach me if you fancied sticking around a bit…'

'Sounds interesting…'

'And you go back to your family and look to the future with a lighter conscience. I'm not suggesting you go back to your old way of working around the clock, but find some balance, do the job you must have found some joy in, work alongside your brothers, and still have a life outside of it.'

'You don't know what you're asking...'

She reached out to cup his cheek and looked up into his gaze as she admitted, 'I put my life on hold to care for my mother and it left me like this, lost and alone.'

'You make it sound like your actions were a bad thing, when what you did was incredible.' He gripped her hips, brought her closer. 'Your mother was very lucky to have you. I'm not sure there are many people out there who would put their life on hold so entirely to care for another.'

'People do it all the time.'

'And they deserve the world for it.'

She choked on a laugh, emotion clogging up her throat. 'Now you're being OTT.'

'I'm not. You're a special breed of human, Jessie Rose.'

'Shame my fiancé didn't agree...' It was out before she could stop it, unguarded by his understanding, his high regard for what he saw as her altruism when Adam had seen it so very differently—that her focus on Mum had left him out in the cold.

But then, Joel hadn't lived through it, and it was easier to be supportive when you weren't the one suffering because of it.

'What do you mean?'

She lowered her lashes. She didn't want to go into her relationship with Adam, and she certainly didn't want to go into the whole devastating scene at the pub. Enough pain had been dished out that day.

'Jessie? What happened?'

She shrugged, stuck to what she could admit. 'I told you I had to leave my life in London to look after Mum at home.'

'You did…'

'That meant leaving Adam in the city, and our relationship became hinged on snatched weekends here and there. Phone calls after Mum was in bed at night…it wasn't enough. Not for him at any rate.'

'But he knew what you were going through. He knew about your mother and her prognosis…'

'Yeah, he knew it all.'

'But he should have been supporting you, helping you… What kind of man uses that against you?'

'One who doesn't get enough attention.'

'What is he? A child? You sound like you feel sorry for him.'

'Hell, no,' she scoffed. 'But I was too detached, emotionally and physically.'

He shook his head. 'Your words or his?'

'His…but he was right.'

'The man was a fool. He should have been there for you, not berated you.'

'It doesn't matter anyway. It was right that it ended—he wasn't the man I thought he was, and I certainly wasn't the person he'd supposedly fallen in love with. I'd changed. The happy-go-lucky girl working hard to drive her career, and partying even harder, was long gone.'

'We all have to grow up some time.'

'Some of us sooner than others…'

'So, what happened?'

'We went our separate ways.' She was stating the obvious and skipping over the worst while she was at it, but he didn't need to hear it. 'I sold my share of our flat to him and took on the family home. I've spent the last six months trying to go through Mum's things and clear space for myself but I don't know, the cottage isn't the same without her and I'm not sure where I want to live now.'

'What about your job? Do you want to go back?'

She gave a short laugh. 'And work with my ex? I don't think so.'

He grimaced. 'Fair enough, but it doesn't mean you can't go back to that career if you enjoyed it and it's what you wanted.'

'That's just it, I don't know what I enjoy any more. Part of this break away is about me trying to find out what that is.'

'Well, in that case, I can suggest one or two things that you definitely seemed to enjoy not even an hour or two ago…'

She laughed, feeling lightheaded with the shifting mood, the lustful fire taking out the dregs of torment in his gaze. 'True, I could definitely do with more of that…you've set the bar pretty high though.'

'Oh, the pressure.'

'No, no pressure,' she said seriously, 'just fun, right?'

'*All* the fun…' He stroked her hair back from her face, held her with his searching gaze. 'And you're sure you'd like me to stay on a little longer?'

'More than. Who else is going to teach me to surf and let go?'

He chuckled low in his throat. 'Well, when you put it like that…'

He kissed her thoroughly, breaking off long before she was ready.

'Thank you, Jessie.'

'For what?' she whispered up at him.

'For helping me see what happened in another light.'

'I'd like to think you would've got there yourself, eventually…'

'I'm not so sure. Brendan, my brothers, my sister, my mother…they've all tried, and yet it's you that's made the difference.'

Her heart fluttered up inside her chest, an over-whelming rush of emotion that she didn't want to identify taking hold, and she gave an unsteady smile. 'In which case, I'm going to take that as a compliment and ask you to dinner because I'm positively ravenous.'

And she needed to break this connection before it branded her heart so completely.

Laughing, he tugged her back towards the bed. 'You and me both. Though I'm not sure it's food I want right now…'

'Food first…' she resisted his pull. She needed a chance to reset, to get herself under control '…and then we have all the time in the world to enjoy dessert.'

'I love your thinking.'

Less of the love, Joel.

Only her heart wasn't listening. And it needed to listen because the one thing she'd learned that day was that, as broken as Joel's heart was, it belonged to another.

His wife. His soulmate. His Katie.

And, for all that it hurt, she needed to remember it.

CHAPTER ELEVEN

'Hannah, what's wrong?'

Jessie whisper-blurted down the phone, her body hunched forward as she padded to the bathroom without turning on a light. She didn't want to wake a softly snoring Joel sprawled out in her bed, where he'd spent the last three nights.

She dropped to the toilet seat, squinted against the glare from her phone and clocked the time—three a.m.!

Either Hannah had pocket-dialled her on her morning commute, or something was seriously wrong. Heart thudding in her chest as she started to think the worst, she tried again. 'Hannah?'

'Jessie, it's about time!'

'What is it? What's happened?'

'What do you mean, what's happened? You haven't answered your phone in two days, you're ignoring my messages…you've got me going out of my mind.'

'Hannah, it's three in the morning.'

'*And?* How else am I to get you to pick up the phone?'

Heart ticking at a more normal pace, she leaned back against the toilet. 'Gee, I don't know, Sis.

Tell me you need to speak to me urgently—that ought to work.'

'I did say that.'

'When?'

'When I messaged you yesterday and said we need to talk.'

'What part of that means call me now?'

'It should be obvious.'

Jessie rubbed at her forehead and stifled a yawn. 'Sis, you sent me here to get a life and I've been busy getting one. *Now* you're worrying I'm not available twenty-four-seven.'

'You can have a life *and* message me back.'

Her sister had a point. But she'd been so caught up in Joel and all the fun they'd been having she hadn't paused long enough to think about Hannah and her worrying.

Liar. You've been avoiding having to admit the truth about you and Joel and now she's caught you in bed with him…

'I'm sorry, Sis, you're right. I should have replied sooner.'

'Yes, you should have. What's going on? It's not like you to be so quiet.'

'I'm on holiday, relaxing, doing everything you said I needed to…' She scrunched up her face as she acknowledged she was doing a lot more than that and her sister would be less than happy.

'But Joel is still there, right?'

The hairs pricked on the back of Jessie's neck. 'Yes.'

Hannah went quiet, the elephant on the line very much unavoidable now.

'Look, Hannah, you really don't need to worry about me—I'm having the time of my life.'

'Time of your life alone, or with him?'

'What does that matter?'

'Of course it matters. I didn't send you there to get caught up in a guy, I sent you there to focus on you.'

'And I am focusing on me.'

'So there's nothing going on between the two of you?'

Jessie looked through the gap in the door, to the moonlight casting shadows over his sleeping form, and turned away. She couldn't lie to Hannah, but neither did she need her playing the big-sister card right now.

'Nothing that will last longer than my time here.'

'What's that supposed to mean?'

'It means I'm having a great time, which was the whole point of this trip, right?'

'But—he's not—he's not in a good way, Jessie.'

'And what would you know about it?'

'He's not right.'

She gave a soft huff. 'You make him sound like some axe murderer!'

'He has more baggage than a Boeing 747 and

I don't like that you're alone out there with him. Not with his reputation and...'

'A reputation handcrafted by the press.'

'And his family and his friends... You know he's a widow?'

'Yes.' Jessie swallowed the sadness and the pang of envy that came unbidden. She had no right to be jealous of a woman whose life had been so cruelly cut short. But witnessing his undying love for Katie...she couldn't think of it without hurting too. 'He's been through a lot.'

'And he's never recovered, Jessie.'

'He's getting better, I can tell...'

'How? You've known him five minutes.'

Jessie shook her head. Her sister wouldn't understand. Jessie wouldn't believe it either if she hadn't lived it—sharing so much, *feeling* so much in such a short space of time.

'And you don't know him at all.'

'I know that he ran from his life when his wife died two years ago and that he's still running. Bedding half the female population while he's at it.'

'Hannah!' It wasn't like her sister to believe in gossip and she didn't need to hear it. She knew there was no future with Joel and she didn't need her sister sticking the knife in any deeper. 'That's not fair.'

'Isn't it?'

'You don't know any of this for a fact.'

'Are you saying that he hasn't? And why are you defending him?'

She nipped her lip, unable to tell her sister the truth because that would mean acknowledging it herself. That she was falling for him and she had no idea how to stop herself...other than to end it now, and she wasn't prepared to do that.

'Look, honey, this isn't some fairy-tale romance like in one of your books...'

'Seriously, Sis...' Jessie choked out, needing her to stop.

'Seriously what? I know you and your good heart. I know it'll be breaking at what he went through, and I know you'll want to help heal him. Of all the men to put in your path, he's your catnip, but he'll leave you high and dry. Mark my words, he'll—'

'Will you stop, Han?' She tried to laugh it off. 'You're being utterly ridiculous! Have you been drinking?'

'As if. It's eight in the morning here.'

'And still, I'm asking. Maybe I should check in with Leon—is he there?'

'Leon?'

'No, the tooth fairy... Hannah?'

'He's—he's extended his trip to LA.'

Okay, so that was news. 'How long for?'

'I don't know.'

'You don't know?'

'No. I don't know, Jessie. Now stop changing the subject.'

How could her sister not know when her husband would return? She got that their careers came first, but still...and was it her imagination, or the lateness of the hour, or was the defensive shoe on the other foot now?

'Is everything okay at home, Han?'

'It will be when you put my mind at rest.'

Back to the attack, then...

'Just tell me I'm wrong, Jessie, and I'll leave you to enjoy your holiday in peace.'

She stood up and paced to the shower, pressed her hot forehead to the cool tiles. 'Like I said, you don't need to worry about me. As for Joel, I know what I'm doing.'

Silence. Then, 'You sure about that, love? Are you *sure* you know what's going on behind the charm he's bound to be showing you?'

'Yes.'

Because she did. He'd opened up to her. Exposed his deepest regrets, his weaknesses, his undying love for his late wife. He couldn't have been any clearer that there was no future here.

'You won't be able to change him, Jessie, you know that, don't you?'

'Who said anything about changing him?'

'You know what I mean.' Hannah sighed down the phone. 'Do you know his sister has an engagement party coming up in New York and he hasn't even RSVP'd? Brendan's been tasked with making sure he gets there, but seriously, who even does that to their own sister?'

'He'll have his reasons.'

Reasons Jessie understood even if she disagreed, but it wasn't her place to tell Hannah of them.

'Reasons that justify the stress he's putting them all under.'

'You don't understand, Sis.'

'Well, Brendan says—'

'*Brendan* should spend more time being a friendly ear to Joel than criticising him to you and trying to control him from afar.' She was pained, angry, frustrated at her sister's interference when all she wanted to do was enjoy this borrowed time with Joel.

'That's hardly fair.'

'No. What's not fair is you ruining the best thing to ever happen to me.'

She cut the call. Stared at the phone burning a hole in her palm. How dared Hannah? How very dare she?

And, oh, God, what had she just said?

'Is everything okay?'

She spun on the spot to see Joel in the doorway. Clad in black briefs, hair all mussed, a frown on his sleep-flushed face, he'd never looked more beautiful…or had her heart racing so fast. Her words echoed in her ears:

No, what's not fair is you ruining the best thing to ever happen to me.

Had he heard her?

Please don't let him have heard her…

'Sorry.' She gave him a weak smile. 'Did I wake you?'

'Only when I reached out and you weren't there.'

Her heart warmed, her pulse eased—maybe he hadn't heard her…

She closed the distance between them, took hold of his hand and kept on walking. 'Let's put that right.'

'Who was on the phone?'

Her step faltered and she prayed he didn't notice. 'Just my sister.'

'Did she forget the time difference?'

Releasing his hand, she pulled back the bed sheet and climbed in. 'No, she just forgot I'm a grown-up.'

He got in beside her. 'Want to talk about it?'

She curved her palm around his neck, looked up into his dark, glittering gaze and slowly dragged her mouth over his, using the tantalising contact to take out the remnants of cold.

'No. I just want you.'

For so long as I can have you…

Joel let her kiss him, let her mould her body to him as she urged him to lie back…

But he couldn't quit the nagging voice in the corner of his mind repeating her words back at him:

'What's not fair is you ruining the best thing to ever happen to me.'

It didn't have to be about him. About them. It could be anything.

He'd only been in her life a short while. And yes, things between them were incredible, passionate, intense…but *best thing ever*? That suggested something with longevity, something more than just great sex, a great connection…a relationship?

No, they weren't going there. She knew that. He knew that.

But what if she'd changed the parameters on him, what if she was starting to develop feelings for him, what if…?

'Are *you* okay?' She pressed up on his frozen chest, the moonlight highlighting the deep groove between her brows and the worry in her eyes.

He cleared his throat. 'More than…'

Combing his fingers through her hair, he brought her in for a kiss—sweet, savouring, tantalising… now wasn't the time to talk about it, she'd already told him that.

That's right, blame her, and run from it. Just like you always do.

He clenched his eyes shut on the inner disdain, rolled her under him, kissed her deeper. Kissed her until the voice gave up and the passion took over. This was a wave he could willingly ride…

Facing reality and what was happening beneath the surface, that was a work in progress.

But at least he'd *agreed* to make progress on it, to return to his business and the family fold.

Thanks to Jessie.

And he could only hope to give her enough in return. To help her experience new things, let go and have fun.

It was a start…as for the end, that was a problem for another day.

Healing and moving forward was one thing. Asking for a repeat of a love lost…only a fool did that.

And he was no fool.

CHAPTER TWELVE

'JOEL, STOP…STOP!' Jessie blurted between giggles, shoving his hands from her hips. 'I'm done!'

'You sure?' He tugged her out of the shallows, swept her wet hair back from her face. 'You almost had it.'

'I've fallen in too many times to count.'

'Everyone wipes out at some point, even the pros…'

'But you make it look easy.'

'I've had plenty of practice, which is just what you need. And I'm not done watching you surf yet…it's quite the aphrodisiac.'

And he wasn't lying. Watching the wide-eyed fear shift into narrow-eyed determination into creased-up joy and laughter had been mesmerising.

'Whatever! Flattery isn't going to get me back out there again today.'

'No…' he pulled her in close '…what about this?'

Pouring the passion she'd inspired into the move, he kissed her until she softened in his arms, a whimper rising in her throat.

'Playing dirty, Joel.' Her eyes were hooded, her voice husky.

'I prefer to call it adding to the fun.'

'Fun?' She laughed as she palmed his chest. 'How's wiping out fun?'

'Wiping out *is* part of the fun.'

'Tell that to my bruised limbs.'

'I will tell each and every one as I tease them back to health later.'

'Is that a promise?'

'It is…if you get back out there.'

She shook her head, laughed some more. 'You're a hard taskmaster.'

'And you're a good pupil…when you do as I say.'

'Like I did with the rope swing?'

He grimaced. 'Okay, so I made a very slight misjudgement there but all's well that ends well. The water softened the blow.'

'Not to my bruised ego, it didn't! And I think you did it on purpose to get me out of my clothes… again.'

He held his hands up. 'Can I help it if I love you in clothes as much as I do out of them?'

Her eyes sparkled up at him, her cheeks flushing a delicate shade of pink and highlighting the freckles sprinkled across her nose. He dipped to press the lightest of kisses there, felt his heart pulse in his chest…and the swift echo of panic.

Jessie was getting to him, touching that part of

him he'd promised to keep locked away, but when he saw how much she was changing with his help, he was powerless.

A week they'd spent living their best lives, to use Jessie's words. She'd fulfilled her promise to try new things, to let go and do things she'd never dreamed of doing.

And the more they experienced together, the deeper the feelings burrowed...

'You going to get all poetic again and talk about me spreading my wings?'

He chuckled, stroked her cheek as he admitted, 'I was never one for poetry, you obviously bring it out in me.'

'We bring a lot out in each other...'

He searched her gaze, desperately seeking the answer to an unsaid question, his mind telling him this wasn't the plan, his heart not listening. The ocean lapped around them, the board attached to her ankle bobbing several feet away. Time was passing and he wanted to hit 'pause'. Trap this moment, indulge it, then move on, unmarked, unaffected, whole...or as whole as he could ever be without Katie.

But this past week with Jessie...that aching, gaping hole inside hadn't felt so vast.

Her lashes fluttered, breaking the connection first. 'We should probably head back in anyway, dinner won't be long.'

'We should.'

She started to move off and he tugged her back in for a kiss because kissing her was far easier than dwelling on the shifting tide inside…or the reminder that he would be walking away from her very, very soon.

Jessie tried to let herself be consumed by his kiss, sensing the urgency and desperation in it and wondering at its cause.

Was it the same reason she'd broken the connection with the mention of dinner? Was he getting too caught up in whatever this was between them? Was he losing sight of the deal they'd made—a fling, a bit of fun, nothing more?

And if so, what did that mean?

The board tugged at her ankle, its presence as annoying as the racing questions that wouldn't stop long enough to just be, and she pressed him away.

'As much as I want to kiss you for ever and a day, I need to be free of this board.'

He chuckled, though it sounded edgy to her ears, and raked a hand through his hair that had curled and crisped with the salt of the sea. 'Let me help you with that.'

He ducked to unstrap her and she rested a hand on his shoulder, felt the heat of his skin, the strength beneath her palm…

'You know if we're quick,' she murmured, 'we might have time for some pre-dinner fun.'

He yanked the board up. 'You're on.'

And the fun was everything she'd anticipated and more. The race back to the house had been scuppered twice. Once by a grinning Paolo with a knowing look in his eye. Twice by a severe-looking Anton, who pressed his lips together and let his eyes do the talking for him. He wasn't happy. Which likely had more to do with his boss than anything else.

She'd feel sorry for him if it weren't for the fact that the thing bringing him so much displeasure was giving her *all* the pleasure.

She smiled into the mirror as she fastened one crystal chandelier earring—they were a statement accessory for sure, but tonight she felt like making a statement. Her confidence was right up there, blossoming under Joel's lavish care.

'Wow!'

The man himself appeared in the bathroom doorway, towel around his hips, hair all wet, eyes and grin all for her. 'Is it a special occasion?'

She met his eyes in the mirror, her smile lifting further. 'No occasion, I just fancied making an effort. It's Friday night after all.'

'Is it? I never keep track of the days when I'm away.'

'I get the feeling you haven't kept track of the days in a long time.'

Something passed over his expression and she knew she'd hit on the truth, but the look was gone as quickly as it had come, replaced by his classic lop-sided grin. 'Are you going to get at me for my wastrel ways again, because you remember how that argument ended the last time?'

'Not at all…though now you mention it.'

She stood and smoothed down her floor-length dress, the black fabric fitting her curves like a glove, the low V-neck designed to draw the eye, and it had certainly captured his, their hungry depths lighting a fire within that was never far from being stoked in his presence.

'I quite liked where that—' Her phone buzzed to life on the dressing table, cutting her words short, and she glanced at the screen, to the message all lit up. 'Oh, dear.'

'What is—?'

Joel's phone chimed in beside the bed and he crossed the room, lifted it, his grimace a mirror image of hers.

'Let me guess,' she said. 'Brendan?'

He nodded and gestured to hers. 'Let me guess, your sister?'

She nodded and he tossed his phone aside, stepped towards her.

'Warning you off me?'

She hummed. 'Telling you to steer clear?'

He hummed. 'It's becoming something of a regular occurrence.'

'Do you think Anton's reporting everything back?'

'Well, not quite everything…he's not inside these four walls for a start.'

She laughed softly, the gesture hitching as his hands came around her.

'It kind of makes it a little more thrilling, don't you think?'

'What?' She hooked her hands around his neck, savouring the heat of his body, the clean masculine scent of his skin. 'A touch of the forbidden?'

'*All* of the forbidden.' He nipped at her lip and she gave a husky chuckle.

'You really are trouble.'

'With a capital T. Are you complaining?'

'Hell, no.'

Because she wasn't. Life had never been so electrifying, so energising, so all-consuming. Even her nightmares were a distant memory with Joel sharing her bed.

And what about when he isn't? When this holiday, this break from reality, is over and you return to your cosy cottage in your quiet village, with your nine-to-five job, whatever that might be, no mum to care for and Hannah living her best life in London?

She shot it all down. It was a worry for another day. Besides, Joel had taught her the joy she could find in new pursuits, pursuits she could continue back home. Surfing, paddleboarding, rock-climbing…

All without him…?

'Are you going to put some clothes on…' she stroked her palms down his chest, smothering the prickle of panic with the thrill of his pecs rippling beneath her caress '…or are you planning on dining like this?'

'I think Anton's already irked enough without serving me dinner in a towel.'

'Do you think he really is irked, or is he just projecting his boss's displeasure?'

'A bit of both, I reckon.'

'What is Brendan's problem anyway? Surely as your best friend he should be happy you're… you know…'

'Moving on with my life?'

'Yes.'

'I think he thinks I've been moving on with it just a little too much.'

She frowned up at him. 'That's only because you've been on the run for so long. When you return to your family and work…' He tensed beneath her touch, moving away to toss his towel on the bed where he'd left his clothes for the evening.

'What?' She wrapped her arms around herself, goosebumps prickling in his sudden absence. 'What's wrong?'

'Nothing.' He thrust one leg into his trousers, then the other, fastened them up far more sharply than necessary. 'Just one thing at a time, yeah?'

'But you said, we agreed…'

He pulled on his shirt, buttoning it. 'I know, and

I will, but it's going to take time. I'm not about to walk back in and pretend none of it ever happened.'

'No one's expecting you to. But your sister's engagement party is coming up, maybe that would be a good place to start?'

He froze. 'How'd you know about that?'

'Hannah mentioned it.'

'When?'

'When I spoke to her.'

His eyes narrowed sharply, their piercing depths chilling her to the core. 'You've been talking about me? My family?'

'No—no, not like that.' A shudder ran through her, the colour draining from her face as she sensed where this was heading, the raw nerve she had inadvertently touched... 'It's not like that... please, Joel, listen to me. It came up in conversation. She was concerned that you hadn't responded to your sister's—'

A rap on the door had their heads snapping in its direction.

'Yes,' she called out, her eyes returning to his, her heart wary.

Anton cleared his throat on the other side. 'Dinner is served.'

'Thank you, Anton.' She tried to sound jovial. 'We'll be there in a second.'

His footsteps retreated, the silence stretched.

'Joel, I—'

'You go,' he ground out. 'I've lost my appetite.'

'Please, Joel…' she reached for him, though he was too far away and she daren't step towards him in case he fled altogether. 'Hannah was— she was trying to help. Your sister's upset that you haven't replied, and they want you in New York…they all do.'

'And your sister thinks she has the right to interfere, to get you to interfere…'

'No, Joel, that's not what—'

'Leave it, Jessie.'

'But we need to talk about this.'

'No. We don't.'

And then he left her, alone and dressed to the nines to endure dinner for one while she came to terms with the pressing realisation that she was already losing him. And she wasn't ready for that…

But would she ever be?

CHAPTER THIRTEEN

JOEL STALKED AWAY from the bedroom, his scowl as dark as the clothes he'd thrown on. He wasn't in any mood for dinner. Wasn't in any mood for anything but his own company.

This was why he didn't get close to people. People who could pass judgement, question his behaviour, make him feel like this…

Of course Jessie had been talking to her sister about him. Hell, he'd been standing there when they'd been talking about him. Been there when Hannah had messaged her about him too.

But this felt different. This was about his family. His obligations. And they were no one else's business but his own.

Until you failed to respond to Simone's RSVP and made it everyone else's business.

His mother, his brothers, Brendan and now Jessie via Hannah, all applying pressure for him to wake up to his responsibilities as the head of the family. The man expected to fill in for their father, to toast their engagement and give away his sister.

He raked a hand through his hair, felt the guilt weigh his legs down and slow his pace. He was the one in the wrong, and yet here he was running from Jessie, taking it out on Jessie.

The only person he should be angry with, frustrated with, was himself.

Not Jessie, the one woman who understood him better than anyone. The one woman who had intervened because she cared.

Cursing aloud, he did an about-turn and retraced his steps.

He found the bedroom deserted, her signature perfume still hanging in the air, creating a trail that led him to the dining room, where Anton was helping her into her seat.

She started when she saw him, her eyes widening, her cheeks flushing. If not for their audience, he was sure she'd say something too, but instead she pursed her lips, avoided his eye.

He gave Anton a nod and took the seat opposite, waited quietly while the wine was poured and Margot brought out the dishes.

'Tonight we have a pineapple rum-glazed chicken with a rainbow slaw and chilli-salted watermelon.'

He took up his wine. 'Thank you, both.'

'Yes, thank you—tell Vittorio it looks delicious.'

He wondered if everyone else could tell that Jessie's voice was unusually subdued. Subdued and sad, and it was all his fault. His grip around the glass pulsed as he raised it to his lips, his eyes fixed on her and the damage he'd caused.

'Bon appétit!'

He jumped at Anton's exclamation, masking it with the flicker of a smile as he watched the man usher Margot out with him.

The silence stretched. Deafening. Disorientating. They were never this quiet together. Ever.

She reached for her glass, took a slow sip.

'I'm—' he started.

'Can I—?' she said over him.

'You go,' they said in unison, and she cracked the smallest of smiles, the sight a blessed relief.

He dipped his head. 'Ladies first...'

She took a hesitant breath. 'I wanted to explain, my sister and I haven't been gossiping about you and your family or your past. She was worried about us spending so much time together. I'm her little sister and she forgets that I'm a grown-up, quite capable of making my own decisions and deciding who I spend time with.'

He nodded, absorbing her words... 'She's just trying to protect you.'

'Precisely. She only brought up the engagement party and your lack of reply because Brendan has obviously mentioned it and it adds to her concern over your...your state of mind.'

He swallowed his wine with difficulty. 'I guess I deserve that.'

She shook her head, her blue eyes earnest as she stared back at him. 'But she doesn't know you like I do.'

'And you think you know me…' It wasn't really a question.

'I think I do,' she whispered, and, rather than recoil, his body warmed. Craving her. Her comfort, her care, her passion. All things that he shouldn't—*couldn't*—want without giving away that part of him reserved for his wife.

The pain in his chest deepened. Guilt. The inevitability of a return to reality. The suffocating realisation that he couldn't do anything about it. He couldn't control it. No more than he could control how he felt about the beautiful, compassionate woman sitting across the table from him.

'What did you want to say?' she asked.

He clenched his teeth, drew a breath through his nose. He owed her this.

'I wanted to say I'm sorry.' It came out gruff, rough, his voice failing to hold the power he wanted it to, and he cleared his throat. 'I took my anger out on you when I should be taking it out on myself.'

'What makes you say that?'

'Because I'm a selfish idiot. I've been protecting myself for so long, avoiding reality, that I've been ruining the lives of those around me.'

Her brows drew together. 'I don't think it's as bad as all that…'

'Don't you?' he blurted. 'You've been pretty vocal on it.'

'I was—I was only trying to help, Joel.'

'I know,' he said, softer now, realising he'd been too blunt. 'And you have helped, so don't make light of my actions now. I've been an arse. My sister's getting married and probably wants to ask me in person to give her away. Instead, I've been so self-absorbed in my grief, I've not responded to the invitation for her celebration—I haven't even congratulated her face-to-face. What big brother behaves like that?'

Her lashes fluttered and she wet her lips, unwilling or unable to answer. In either case, he knew he was right.

'You see, I have been listening. To you, my family, Brendan…it's all going in.'

She nodded, her eyes going to her glass where she traced the condensation with her fingers.

What was she thinking? Was she holding back like he was? Keeping a lid on the feelings trying to claw their way out?

He wanted to thank her for so much. For asking him to spend the last few weeks with her. For the joy she had brought him, the experiences they'd shared, the chance to feel again…but how could he say any of that without strengthening the bond between them?

A bond that would encourage more…more than he could ever freely give.

He'd seen it in her eyes when he'd walked away from her in the bedroom. The pain he had inflicted, the feeling that had to exist for her to feel such pain…

Love.

And she couldn't love him, no more than he could ever love her.

'Everyone makes mistakes, Joel.' Her gaze lifted to his, her blue eyes bright in the candle-light and filled with it all.

'Even you?' Ants marched over his skin as he threw the focus back on her and not the future she so clearly wanted to discuss.

'Even me.' She gave a soft laugh. 'What matters is how we learn from them and move on.'

'If you're going to bring up how you neglected your fiancé again then I'm sorry, that's not going to cut it. He was the selfish idiot, not you.'

'No, I wasn't referring to that.'

'Really?' He tried to inject teasing into his tone. 'So just what little misdemeanour did Jessie Rose commit?'

'No one's perfect, Joel.'

'No, but on the human imperfection scale you're definitely at the other end to me.'

She scoffed, the spark in her eye the same as the determined glint she bore every time she tried popping up on the surfboard. 'You didn't meet me when I was younger.'

He chuckled, took a sip of wine, easing into the conversation that was so much easier when it focused on her past rather than his own. 'How young? Are we talking tantrum-throwing toddler, truant-playing schooler, rebellious teen…?'

He was trying to imagine her through the ages…

'Try all of the above.'

'I don't believe you.'

'It's true.' She sipped her wine, the spark in her eye now a full-on sparkle. 'You ask Hannah. She took the brunt of it, covering for me with Mum, supervising me when she'd rather have been studying, saving me from school expulsion and boys that were up to no good.'

'Ah, so some things don't change.'

'No.' The spark fizzled out. 'But I'm not a defiant child or rebellious teen any more, and I don't need her protection. I thought things would change. For years I tried to prove myself to her, followed her to London, got a good job, a guy who on the face of it was good for me, and then I stepped in when Mum needed us too.'

'But she still treats you the same…'

'And it drives me crazy.'

'Old habits die hard, I guess.'

She gulped on her wine. 'Well, this habit is long past its expiry date.'

'So, tell her.'

'I've tried.'

'Tell her again until she gets it. Keep being you until she gets it. One day she'll have to see you for the strong, independent, amazing woman that you are.'

She stilled, wine glass pausing mid-air. 'Is that truly how you see me?'

Damn it, too much, Joel. Too much sentiment. Too much honesty.

But he couldn't take it back, nor did he want to. She needed to see herself how others should see her, how he saw her…

'Yes.' He broke the eye contact before she could read too much in his gaze. 'Now we should eat before this gets cold.'

She didn't move, her eyes staying fixed on him. 'Thank you.'

'For what?'

She gave the smallest of shrugs. 'For being you.'

He gave a tight laugh. 'So you accept my apology and we're friends again?'

She gave a half smile but the look in her eye stole his breath away.

'Always.'

Jessie was floating on air. The roller coaster of having Joel walk away from her only to come back and tell her how he felt…well, not quite how he felt, but how he saw her with all that passion and encouragement.

How could she not believe it meant more? How could she not wonder if he felt the same as her? That for all he loved his late wife, there could be room for her too?

There was only one way to find out…

If she was to come away from this trip with no regrets, she had to tell him the truth. She had to tell him that she was in love with him…even if it meant pushing him away all together.

'Do you fancy a nightcap?' he asked, rising from the table after the plates had been cleared and offering her his hand.

'I don't think I should—that wine has gone straight to my head.'

Along with your words…

She smiled up at him, slipping her hand into his and feeling the familiar warmth spread from her palm to her heart.

'That'll be all the exercise and fresh air.'

She laughed. 'Perhaps.'

'Bed, then?'

She nodded, letting him lead the way. They passed Anton in the hall and bade him goodnight, sending thanks to both Vittorio and Margot.

'Do you think he'll ever get over the fact we are together?'

'I think he'd be happier if we *were* together…'

By some miracle Jessie kept her stride smooth, her breathing less so. Joel hadn't looked at her as he'd said it, hadn't witnessed the way his simple statement had shattered her heart like a pick through ice.

But what could she do? She was in love with a man still in love with another, and there wasn't anything she could do about it.

They entered the bedroom and she headed straight for the dressing room, her fingers trembling as she fumbled over the zip at the back of her dress.

Joel came up behind her. 'Let me help you...'

Silently she turned to face the mirrored wardrobe, sweeping her hair to the side to grant him access, her eyes on him, her heart aching in her chest. Could he learn to love her too? Given time? Given a chance...?

He stepped closer, his fingers grazing the delicate skin of her neck as he dipped to press a kiss there, and her breath caught.

'It's almost a crime to take you out of this,' he murmured, his head still bowed as he lowered the zip. 'It's beautiful on you.'

His eyes lifted to hers in the mirror, their dark and hungry depths seeing off any reply as he smoothed his hands beneath the fabric and eased it over her shoulders.

It fell to the floor in a whisper of silk and she made no attempt to stop it. She trusted him to see her naked beneath the spotlights. He'd already traced every freckle she'd once hated as a child, kissed every scar, the birthmark on her left hip, the mole on her shoulder...he'd made her feel loved whether he'd intended to or not.

And now she was baring her all to him. Both physically and mentally, and God help them both, he needed to know it.

'On second thoughts,' he dipped to her ear, his breath sending a thrilling shiver running through her as he unhooked her bra, 'you look amazing out of it too.'

The lace joined her dress on the floor and his hands smoothed over her front, tantalising her nerve-endings, making her shift against him as her body craved more. 'You are exquisite, Jessie.'

She took a shuddery breath, raised her hands behind her head to hold him to her and spoke before the courage left her. 'Exquisite enough to keep me?'

He stilled, his eyes colliding with hers—shock, distress, a dizzying torment within the fire. 'Don't ask me that.'

She turned in his arms. 'Why?'

Blue eyes blazing against cheeks streaked with carnal heat, he ground out, 'You know why.'

'I know you've been hurt, that life took away your one true love, but you know what…' she held his gaze, knowing what she was risking and doing it all the same '…it doesn't mean there can't be another. You may not see me as your soulmate, but we have something special, Joel. I'm as sure of that as I am of you and the man you are.'

'I can't, Jessie.' His hands upon her skin trembled with his words. 'I can't go through that again.'

'Why?'

'Because that pain…' The breath he took was hoarse, his cheeks paling, the torment taking out the fire in his gaze '…that pain is enough to cripple you.'

'It crippled you and you've come back from it.' She held fast, knowing she had to, willing away his pain, willing to replace it with what she could give him.

'And I'm *still* coming back from it. I don't know if I'll ever come back from it. If I'll ever feel normal again.'

'And what's normal, Joel?' She stroked her fingers through his hair as she sought to soothe the anguish in his eyes.

'I don't know. I just know it's not this.'

'This?'

'You and me. This alternative world we've lived in—this isn't reality.'

'But it can be.'

He was shaking his head, withdrawing from her, the distance more acute for his proximity, and the chill of the air-con provoking every raised hair down her back. But now wasn't the time to back down—she'd started this and she owed it to herself to finish it. She owed it to them.

She owed it to her mother, whose advice had never felt more applicable as she repeated it for his benefit now...

'Life is the adventure you make it, Joel—live it, love it, no regrets.'

He barked out a laugh that cut right through her. 'You think throwing fancy memes at me will change my mind?'

She paled, chilled to the bone. 'No...' Her voice

cracked. 'My mother told me that before she died because she—she felt I needed to hear it. And if she were still alive, she'd think the same of you too.'

She stepped away, never more aware of the epic mistake she had made and needing to be out of his orbit, needing layers, so many layers…she was done being laughed at by the men in her life.

He reached for her. 'I'm sorry, Jessie, I didn't mean to—I didn't realise… I wasn't making a mockery of your mother…or you! I'm so sorry.'

But she was done listening, done feeling. She drifted to the bed and pulled the sheets up high, turning away from him, desperate to ignore the entire world. Hannah. Adam. Joel. Everyone and everything.

'I'm sorry,' he said, coming up behind her. 'If I'd known your mother had said it, I never would have laughed. I'm sorry. But you, this, us, I thought you knew…we agreed what this was.'

'You're right, we agreed.' Her voice was monotone.

'*Please*, Jessie.' She felt the bed dip with his weight, his hand gentle on her hip, but she refused to turn. 'I can't bear to hurt you too.'

'You didn't,' she said to the opposite wall. 'I did it to myself.'

And more fool you…

CHAPTER FOURTEEN

JOEL WOKE WITH a start.

What in the…?

The room was in darkness, the moonlight painting shadows and accentuating his black clothing against the white sheets. Why was he fully clothed and why did his cheek throb?

He rubbed against the sensation, adjusted his jaw, the night's events replaying with swift and sickening precision.

Jessie.

He looked to her beside him, curled up in the sheets, his heart aching to reach for her but something wasn't right. Her cheeks were flushed and clammy, her hair clinging to her sweat-drenched skin…

Was she ill? It wasn't hot in here, so why was she—?

'Mum… Mum…' She screwed her face up in her sleep, her hands flinging out and he jerked back, grabbing her wrist before she struck him. 'Mum!'

She tugged on his hold, her free hand clawing at her throat, her nails marring her skin, and he cursed, impulse taking over as he grasped it gently and shifted closer, trapping her flailing hands against his chest.

'It's okay, sweetheart,' he murmured, his heart wrenching in his chest as she fought against him and whatever it was that haunted her. 'It's okay. It's okay.'

She wriggled and writhed, choking on thin air, and he tried to stay calm, steady his heart, when all he wanted to do was shake her awake and make everything better.

'It's okay, sweetheart,' he repeated softly. 'It's okay, you're dreaming, you're safe, I've got you.'

He held her in his arms, rocked her as he shushed her. He lost track of time, his focus wholly on her breathing as he willed it to slow, willed her pain to stop.

Eventually she calmed, her body sagging in his hold, her breath evening out.

He pressed a kiss to her hair. 'It's okay,' he repeated, though this time he wasn't sure who he was telling—himself or her. 'Everything will be okay.'

Because it would be. He'd make damn sure of it.

Her head nudged his chin and he looked down. Big, round eyes blinked up at him, piercing his heart. 'Was I dreaming?'

'You were having a nightmare, baby.'

Her lushes fluttered, her throat bobbed. 'Did I...? Did I wake you?'

'It's okay.'

Her gaze drifted to his cheek, their depths flaring at whatever she saw there. 'Did I h-hurt you?'

'No.' He would have laughed if not for the horror in her face.

'But your cheek…'

'What about it?'

'It's…' She swallowed, her voice a whisper. 'It's red.'

'You caught me in your dream, don't—'

'Oh, God, I'm sorry!' She tried to press away from him and he pulled her back.

'Don't say sorry, not to me. I hated seeing you like that…'

She stared back at him, tension pulling her body taut.

'Please, baby, come back to me.'

Slowly she did as he asked, resting her cheek against his chest, but the tension remained, her breathing non-existent. Did her dream still haunt her?

'Do you want to talk about it?'

A second's pause, then, 'My dream?'

He pressed a kiss to her hair. 'If it'll help…'

She blew out a long, slow breath, then, 'It's a nightmare I used to have as a kid…'

She was so quiet he had to strain to hear her over the pounding of his heart. 'And it's only come back now?'

They'd slept together many nights and he'd never been woken by her, not like this.

'No. It started again after Mum died…it comes with my anxiety—the more out of control I feel in my life, the more likely I am to have it.'

Did that mean he'd triggered it? His behaviour that evening?

'Is it the same every time?'

'Pretty much.'

He stroked her hair, trying to ignore the voice within and the pain in his heart.

'I'm being buried alive. I can hear the earth hitting the coffin and scream but no one can hear me. I scratch at the lid but it makes no difference.' She shifted on top of him, one leg hooking between his legs as she seemed to cling to him as an anchor in reality, and he continued to stroke her hair, eager to take away the horrific image… for her and for him. 'When I was a child, Mum would rescue me. I'd call for her and she would appear just when I needed her to, and she'd soothe me awake and make everything right again.'

'I didn't want to wake you. I wasn't sure it was the right thing.'

'You were there for me. That's all I needed.'

But who soothed her awake when she was alone, who would do it when he was gone?

She looked up at him, but he couldn't look at her.

'I've not had the dream since my first night here.'

'The night I saw you in the kitchen?'

She nodded. 'It was the reason I was up getting milk…it was Mum's answer to everything.'

He smiled at the ceiling.

'But I've not needed it since—since you. I think you helped put me at ease again.'

And just like that the smile died, her confession pounding through him. He had helped, right up until last night when he'd set her straight on their future. Or lack thereof.

'Thank you.'

He turned rigid with her soft-spoken gratitude, so unexpected, so undeserved. 'You shouldn't be thanking me.'

'I should—you've helped me and I'm so sorry I hurt you…'

He frowned… *Hurt you?*

'Your cheek?' She gestured to it.

He wanted to choke out a laugh. She was referring to the physical hurt, not the emotional, and he was all about the latter. The pain he'd caused her, not the other way around.

'It's fine.'

Her lashes lowered, her cheeks flamed and she gave a hiccup-cum-sob that had him launching himself up but she pinned him back down, her head stubborn on his chest.

'Jessie?'

She refused to look at him and he hooked his finger beneath her chin, lifted her face to force her to meet his eye. 'What is it?'

She hid beneath her lashes. 'It's nothing.'

'Don't lie to me.'

Slowly she met his eye…

'Tell me.'

She swallowed. 'The—The night Adam and I broke up…'

His gut turned over as he nodded. He didn't want to talk of Adam, didn't want to think of him anywhere near her.

'I caught him talking to his mates, joking with his mates in a bar…'

The colour in her cheeks deepened, her mind reliving whatever came next, and when she failed to say anything more he pressed, 'What about?' Though he could already imagine what was coming, anger a subtle burn low in his gut.

'My night terrors…he—he thought it was funny, you know, check out where she clocked me last night. She looks innocent, boys, but that right hook of hers…'

He couldn't speak. The scene she painted had him frozen in time, wishing he could have been there, wishing he could have swiped the smile off the bastard's face.

'It seemed my neglect as he saw it was reason enough to rip into me with his chums…'

He cursed, the anger bubbling over inside as he gave Adam the label he deserved.

She huffed in what he'd like to think was agreement. 'What I don't understand is why he didn't just end it? Why not tell me how he felt and be done with it?'

'Because I suspect he knew you were too good for him.' He released his hold on her chin to palm her cheek, looked into her eyes as he suppressed the anger towards the faceless man she spoke of so that he could assure her of his words. 'A beautiful, kind woman like you on his arm…there was no way he'd throw that away.'

She gave a soft scoff. 'You reckon?'

'You don't?'

She shrugged it off and he wanted her to take it back, accept it for the truth, but she was already talking.

'That night, back at the flat, he tried to tell me he was sorry, tried to fix things. But I felt like such an idiot. So hurt and betrayed. And then it all came out, the truth about how I'd abandoned him and our relationship, how boring I'd become…but if he'd only been honest with me sooner…if he'd just been man enough…'

'What? You think you could have behaved differently? Stayed together? Are you *kidding*?'

The smallest of smiles touched her lips. 'No. But we could have ended things before he humiliated me so publicly.'

He swallowed past the pain in his chest. 'I'm sorry he put you through that, but you have to know it wasn't your fault. That he was pushing the blame on you to make excuses for his own abhorrent behaviour. He was a jerk. *Is* a jerk.' And then it came to him…the pieces falling into place, her prejudice, her severe reaction to him. 'Tell me something, Jessie...'

'What?'

'Adam and his mates—ex-prep boys by any chance?'

Her cheeks flamed anew and he had his answer. 'Makes sense.'

'I'm sorry.'

He blew out a breath. 'No more sorry, Jessie. It's lucky I don't know him because I swear to God...'

She shook her head, her mouth twitching, the pain in her eyes easing away with the rest of his threat. 'Joel?'

'Yes?'

'Kiss me.'

He stared back at her, his head clouded by their unfinished business, their fight...

'But—'

'*Please*, Joel.'

And so, he did.

He kissed her and lost himself in everything that she was, everything that made her worth so much more than he could ever give. A half-broken version of himself that would always feel his happiness tainted by the love that he'd lost.

Not open to the new love that he'd found.

Joel kissed her slowly, kissed her deeply, kissed her until she was a hot mess all over again. Only this time it was pleasure and pain burning a hole through her. Because she wanted him. Desperately. But inside her heart was breaking and she couldn't stop the tears behind her closed lids.

He took his time, teasing every sensitive inch… he knew her, knew her body too. What she liked, what she loved…he knew her better than Adam ever had, cared for her more as his words had just proved, and she loved him for it.

Biting her lip, she dared to look down at him, her hands clutching at the bedsheets as he eased away her knickers, his mouth hot and teasing over her skin. He tossed the fabric aside, his palms cupping the backs of her thighs as he opened her up to him.

'You're like an addiction, Jessie.'

She whimpered in response, her heart pleading for him, wishing it meant that he'd keep on needing her, wanting her…loving her.

She swapped the bedsheets for his hair, her fingers clutching at him as he kissed and caressed the very heart of her, driving her to the precipice and over the edge. Tears of sadness, of happiness, of ecstasy spilled from her lids, and still he didn't stop. His kisses turning gentle as he rose up over her, taking took his time to trail a path all the way back to her lips.

'Oh, baby, don't cry. Please don't cry. He was an arse, a complete and utter arse.'

She shook her head. How could she tell him the tears weren't for Adam but him?

She couldn't. Not after he'd brought her so

much pleasure. So she kept her eyes clamped shut, felt his thumb sweep away the dampness as he dipped to kiss the bridge of her nose.

'Please, I can't bear it.'

But she couldn't stop. Not when her heart was tearing in two.

'Look at me, baby.'

She shook her head again.

'Please, Jessie.' His agonising groan crushed her. '*Please.*'

She forced her eyes to open, her heart contracting at the anguish she spied in his.

'I'm sorry for what happened to you.' He took a shuddery breath. 'And I'm sorry I can't be the man you need. But you deserve so much better than Adam. So much better than me. You deserve someone unbroken and whole. Someone who can love you so completely. Someone who helps you realise how worthy you are and special and—'

She pressed a finger to his lips, shook her head rapidly. 'Please don't, Joel. If you don't want a future with me, please stop now, because I can't bear to hear you say such things and leave me.'

His eyes wavered. 'I just need you to know, it's not you—'

She choked on a pained laugh. 'Don't you dare finish that sentence.'

'Then what do you want me to do?'

'I want you to make love to me. No more words.'

Because she wasn't lying. She couldn't take it.

Each one triggered a confusing mass of warmth and aching pain and she was done.

She would take this night and any more he could give, and walk away stronger, more determined for it.

At least that was what she told herself as she kissed him and unbuttoned his shirt, her trembling fingers frustratingly slow.

'Let me...'

He climbed off the bed, his eyes not once leaving hers as they projected his own torment, his own confusion, his own distress. And then he was stripped bare and back in bed with her, his arms wrapping around her as he kissed her...

'I just need to say one thing,' he murmured against her lips, his earnest eyes locked in hers and making her chest contract around her beating heart. 'You are special to me, Jessie, I swear it.'

And then he kissed her, forestalling any retort she could give, but there were no words left other than the three he didn't want to hear...

I love you.

Joel couldn't sleep. The sun was creeping over the horizon and beside him Jessie slept, her gentle snore far more peaceful than the panicked beat of his heart.

If he'd needed added confirmation that she'd fallen in love with him, then he'd got it. She hadn't said it. She hadn't needed to.

And, coupled with Brendan's last message going round and round in his head, he couldn't find peace. Wouldn't find peace until he put this right.

Gently, he eased out from beneath her and pulled on his clothes. He paused at the door, took one last look…she was exquisite, her hair a wild mass of red upon the white sheets, her lips softly parted, her skin golden in the rising sun.

She's not some temporary sticking plaster that you can rip off and throw away when you're done, Joel. She's been through enough. This trip was meant to help her, not hurt her. You do that and we are done.

His grip around the door handle pulsed as Brendan's words cut his heart in two…one half begging to return to her side, needing the peace he'd lost these past two years and found in her.

The other half knowing and needing to do right. By her, by Brendan, by Katie.

He hadn't set out to hurt Jessie. He'd set out to bring her joy, happiness, to make her experience the rush that life could bring if you took a little risk. Let go and had fun.

But this wasn't fun any more…not for him and certainly not for her when faced with the reality of their situation.

He needed to make a call.

A call he'd likely regret, but he had to do it all the same.

CHAPTER FIFTEEN

JESSIE WOKE ALONE, Joel's imprint in the mattress long gone. His space cold.

She shivered in spite of the sun beaming through the windows, its height in the sky telling her it was late. She checked the time and did a double take. Almost noon.

She shot up. She couldn't believe how late it was. But then, between her nightmare and Joel's attentive lovemaking, she shouldn't be surprised she'd slept in.

What about Joel though? Had he lain awake afterwards, leaving her as soon as he was sure she was asleep?

Had she scared him so much, he'd left altogether…?

No. No, he couldn't have. Not after their talk, not after all he'd said… He wouldn't. Couldn't. But her gut turned over anyway, and she threw back the sheet, the air-con provoking the goosebumps already rife across her skin.

Refusing to let the panic set in, she pulled on her robe and went in search of him.

She found Anton in the central foyer, checking something on his tablet. 'Good morning, Jessie.'

'Hi, Anton.' She scanned the room, the hallways branching off. 'Have you seen Joel?'

'I believe he had some business to take care of this morning. He should be back in time for dinner tonight.'

'Business?' What business could he have that involved leaving the villa but not the island? Unless it was the business of avoiding her… 'So he's not here?'

'No, I'm afraid not.' She could see the cogs turning behind his astute brown eyes, could imagine him assessing her haphazard appearance and piecing it all together.

'I guess he didn't want to wake me,' she rushed out, more for her benefit than his.

'I imagine so—it was quite early when he left. Can I bring you some breakfast in the garden? It's a lovely day now the skies have cleared.'

She shook her head. She didn't think she could eat a thing. Not until she saw Joel and could settle the anxious churn that was building despite her best efforts to quash it.

'Coffee, perhaps? Tea?'

'No, thank you.' She didn't need caffeine to aggravate her already racing pulse. And now Anton was looking at her with such sympathy she wanted to cry.

Was she someone to be pitied now? Was her mistake so very obvious to everyone around her?

'If you change your mind, do let us know.'

'I will. Thank you.'

She didn't change her mind.

She took a swim until her body protested, tried to read but couldn't keep track of the tale, wandered the grounds with no destination in mind.

She knew she was keeping herself busy, refusing to succumb to the panic as she reminded herself that this was in her control. She'd chosen to embark on a fling with Joel. She'd chosen to let go and enjoy it. Chosen to confess her desire for a future too. And now she'd have to face the consequences.

Even if she hadn't *chosen* to fall in love with him. But who did?

Joel certainly hadn't intended for this to come to more, but the look in his eye, the way he treated her, spoke about her...

She had to hope that for all he said they had no future, it was the same for him.

That despite their agreement to a fling, their hearts had taken their own path and become inextricably linked.

Maybe it was that hope that kept the anxiety attack at bay.

Or maybe it was her efforts to fill her time so completely. But she found herself at the clearing he'd brought her to that very first day. Where they'd shared their first kiss...and the hope built with the memory. Reliving the intense pull, the comfort she'd found talking to him, sharing with him.

She leant back against the same palm and breathed in the picture of calm, the sounds of the sea and the wildlife, and let it soothe the stormy remnants within…

Joel fixed his sights on the villa as they approached and ignored the eyes boring into the back of his head. Even Paolo was unusually quiet…though when the atmosphere within the Jeep was thick enough to cut with a knife, who could blame him?

He swiped a hand across the back of his neck, the air-con doing nothing for his cold sweat and gritted his teeth. Told himself this was for the best, he was doing right…

No sooner had Paolo pulled to a stop than Joel was throwing off his seatbelt. 'Just give me a minute.'

He didn't wait for a response as he launched himself out, his stride and focus on the building and the person within.

Only she wasn't inside…a flash of red to the right caught his eye and he froze as she emerged from the trail that led up into the hillside. Her step was tentative, her cheeks were flushed and her smile…her smile had his heart taking off inside his chest.

'You're back.'

He swallowed. Her voice was soft and exquisite and everything he craved. He fought against the pull, bit back the retort he would have given—

In the flesh, baby—because the time for flirtation was over. It was time to get real.

He pushed his sunglasses into his hair. 'Hi.'

'Why didn't you tell me you were heading out today?'

'You were asleep.'

And you were chicken...

'You could've—'

Movement behind him caught her attention, breaking off her words, and he snapped his head around, relieved to see it was Paolo heading to the rear of the Jeep.

She gave a small wave. 'Hey, Paolo.'

'Miss Rose.' He nodded and carried on as Joel closed the distance between them and took her hand in his, tugging her away.

'We need to talk.'

'We are talking.'

'Properly. Let's go inside.'

She stopped, pulled her hand from his grasp, her frown chipping away at his defences. 'You're acting weird...what's wrong? I know last night unsettled you but...'

'That's enough, Joel.'

Brendan's command sliced through the air, traversing the distance with ease.

'I asked you to wait, Brendan!' Joel desperately threw at him as Jessie spun to face their new arrival.

'Brendan?' she whispered, her confusion mounting, her eyes coming back to Joel, begging him for answers. Answers he wanted to have given *before* he dealt with their new arrivals.

'We've waited too long as it is…' It was clear his friend meant letting him stay in the villa as long as he had…letting him stay and letting Jessie get attached, and Joel cringed inside. 'Hannah needs to use the bathroom.'

'Hannah?' Jessie's eyes snapped back to the Jeep as a blonde woman, all elegance and poise, stepped out. 'Sis! What on earth are you—?'

Jessie's eyes darted over them all and he could see the uncertainty, swiftly masked by excitement, as she rushed forward and wrapped her arms around her sister. 'Are you finally taking a holiday and crashing mine?'

She gave a laugh, but it was high, awkward, and Hannah's returned embrace was stilted at best.

'Are you okay?' Hannah scanned Jessie's face, but in truth Joel wasn't sure who looked worse— Jessie in her confused state, or Hannah with her pinched expression, her shadowed eyes and skin pale beneath the thin veil of make-up. But then, she was worried about her little sister and had every right to be…thanks to him.

'How many times do I have to tell you, I'm fine?' Jessie pressed her away to eye her top to toe. 'You don't look so hot though.'

Hannah's eyes flitted to Brendan, who suddenly looked grey in the late-afternoon sun. 'I really do need the toilet.'

'Sure, sure.' Jessie rushed out, 'I'll show you the—'

'Brendan can show her,' Joel interjected, seeking his chance. 'We need to talk.'

The sooner he could get her alone, the sooner he could get the situation back under his control.

You reckon?

He ignored the inner gibe and looked to Brendan, his eyes communicating the silent message: *I'm doing as you asked. You owe me this at least.*

Brendan gave him a grave nod, his hand lowering to Hannah's back as he gently ushered her towards the house. The protective gesture spoke volumes and he wondered if Jessie had noticed it too as she watched them go, eyes narrowed, concentration creasing up her brow.

He closed the distance between them but her gaze didn't shift.

'Please tell me you didn't tell them to come?'

Now she rounded on him, a sudden fire in her depths and he realised she was putting two and two together and not quite hitting four.

'It's not like that.'

'No....' She crossed her arms. 'What is it like then? You wanted to bring a chaperone along to the party a few weeks late?'

'No, God, no…they were already on their way. I promise.'

'You just expedited it?'

'No. Not really. I guess. Hell, I don't know.'

He scoured his brain for the right words, something that would make everything okay, something that would stop the way his heart was aching. He pocketed his hands to stop them reaching for her, knowing she wouldn't welcome it but wanting to do it all the same.

'I don't know how this happened,' he said, 'it wasn't supposed to go like this.'

'And just what do you think "this" is?'

'You know…' He floundered, and she gave a harsh laugh.

'You can't even say it, can you?'

He stared down at her, wanting with all his worth to pull her to him, to soothe the pain he was inflicting and make everything right. But that would take the one thing he couldn't do.

'Does it really scare you that much?'

Of course it did. To open himself up to that world of pain when he was still piecing himself together from the last. To feel that sense of betrayal running thick in his veins over the woman he had lost, in front of the woman he felt far more for than he should.

'It's more complicated than that, you know it is.'

For a brief second her gaze softened, her lashes fluttering over her glistening blues. 'I know, but it doesn't make it hurt any less… I love you, Joel.'

The world froze with his heart.

'I know you don't want to hear it but I'm telling you anyway. I love you and—'

'Don't, Jessie, please don't…' He couldn't bear

hearing it. Couldn't bear the pain in her gaze, the tears forming when it should be said without fear, without sadness. Not like this and not with him.

The front door opened and Anton appeared. He didn't look in their direction as he started bringing out luggage.

'Are those your bags?' she asked, eyes on Anton now.

'Yes.'

'You're leaving, then?'

'Yes.'

She turned back to him, her blue eyes piercing. 'So—we're done?'

'*We* never were, Jessie. You know that…we agreed.'

She scoffed softly. 'We can all go into something thinking it will work out one way, but life has other ideas. You know that better than most.'

He flinched, her words cutting deep.

'I'm sorry, Joel. I don't want to hurt you. I'm trying to wake you up to what we have. What we could have if you'd only give us a chance.'

He stared at her, long and hard, his brain and heart awash with her words.

'I didn't choose to fall in love with you, Joel. I came here to set myself on a different path, to find out what I wanted from life, and you've helped me with that. I've had so much fun, tried things I wouldn't have attempted if not for you. And you've helped me heal, move on from Adam, believe in myself again, and for that I am so grateful.'

He shook his head, tried to speak but no words would come.

'You also made me feel special.' She gave a rueful smile. 'You opened my eyes to the positive rather than the negative. Made me realise that I am strong enough, independent enough to stand up to Hannah, to take control of my life again.' She gave a pitched laugh, the fire returning through the tears. 'But you know what really stings?'

He frowned, unable to respond, unable to shake his head even.

'After all you said, the way that you encouraged me, you've treated me no better than she has.'

He came up sharp. 'What's that supposed to mean?'

'Well, I assume she's here to pick up all the Jessie pieces and put them back together again after your departure, because I couldn't possibly do it on my own.'

'No, that's not—'

'Poor little Jessie, got her heart broken and needs to be looked after all over again.'

'No, Jessie, that's not true. Yes, I wanted you to have someone here. Yes, I wanted to know you were…' His voice trailed off as he realised where he was heading.

'Taken care of?' Her brows nudged skyward, her guess on point.

But it's only because I care, he wanted to scream, *I care too much.*

'Well, you don't need to worry. I'm perfectly capable of taking care of myself and facing my future... I only wish you could say the same.'

She stalked past him, all fire and ice, and everything he'd come to admire, to cherish.

'Your bags are ready, sir,' Anton said as she disappeared inside, his voice lacking its usual warmth.

Brendan appeared in Jessie's place, his murderous expression too much for Joel to bear as he approached.

'Look, I get that you're pissed with me, but can you just...?' He broke off. Brendan didn't just look angry, he looked drawn, his eyes weary and worried and everything in between. 'What's wrong?'

Taking an unsteady breath, his friend raked a hand through his usually well-groomed hair. 'Now isn't the time.'

'What's going on?'

His friend had never been this on edge and he got the distinct impression it wasn't all down to him...for a change.

'Hannah doesn't need this right now.'

'None of us do.'

'You have no idea, believe—'

A woman's sob reached them from inside and instinct kicked in, Joel's legs striking out in their direction, but Brendan placed a palm on his chest. 'No. Leave them.'

'But Brendan...'

'Do you love her?'

His gut rolled, his skin prickled. 'I can't, Brendan, you know that. I can't.'

'Then turn around and leave.'

'But I can't just—'

'You can because it's the right thing to do and you know it too.'

'If this is the right thing, then why does it feel so wrong?'

'Only you can answer that, Joel.'

Jessie stared at Hannah.

Her sister never sobbed. Ever.

Oh, she'd cried when Mum passed, at her bedside and the funeral. But she couldn't think of a single time she'd witnessed her sister outright sob and, like...*ugly* cry.

'You need to get a grip, Sis. I'm fine. Honestly, I'm fine.'

She was surprised at how much she meant it. She was shaky, sure, but she wasn't about to have an attack. For all she hurt, she was in control and that was huge. Her time with Joel, the way he'd boosted her confidence and opened her eyes to who she was, he'd got her to this point.

And even her love for him had given her an inner strength that she hadn't possessed before, fighting for what she wanted, what she believed in, and, as strange as it sounded, it was holding her together.

But what about Joel? Had she made an epic mistake? Pushing him before he was ready, pushing him when he hadn't worked through his grief and his guilt, breaking their agreement by asking for more...?

Yes, she'd done it out of love, but did that really make it okay?

What if she'd set him back? What if she'd caused more damage than good? What if she'd ruined all his progress and he refused to go back to his family now...?

She thought of his stricken face, the desperation in his pleading blue eyes, the damage her words had done, and almost back-pedalled, out through the door and into his arms...not that he wanted her there.

But she would've done it anyway if Hannah hadn't chosen that moment to let out another almighty wail.

'Jesus, Han, calm down. Everything's fine, I promise.'

'No, it's not fine, nothing is.'

'So, I fell in love with the wrong guy, again—it's not the end of the world! I don't need you to sort me out, okay? I'm quite capable of doing that myself.' She was getting angry, frustrated all over again. Did her sister really think she was so weak that she had to travel all this way to make sure she didn't have another breakdown and give herself a breakdown in the process? 'I know you're worried about me, but this has to stop. I'm a fully grown adult, capable of making my own mistakes and learning from them.

I don't need you protecting me all the time, smothering me and mollycoddling me. I don't need—'

'I know you are, Jess!' Hannah shook her head rapidly, cutting her off. 'I'm sorry I've made you feel that way.'

Okay, so if her sister knew that, then why was she here and why was she crying as if the end of the world was nigh? Unless...this wasn't about her at all.

'You're really starting to worry me, Han. What's going on?'

Her sister gave another sob and this time she didn't stop, her body folding in on itself and Jessie shot forward to support her—shock, confusion, a desperate need to comfort her blocking out all else.

'Hey, hey, it's okay…' She hugged her sister to her chest. 'Shh, honey, whatever it is, I'm sure it's okay…just talk to me.'

Hannah burrowed her head into her shoulder. 'You really don't need this right now…'

'That's where you're wrong, Sis. For the first time in your life, you need me and I'm here. This is *everything* I need right now, believe me.'

Because she would be fine. Jessie knew it deep down. Whether Joel would be was another matter, but he had Brendan with him and Hannah needed her. Not the troublesome teen or the adult trying to prove her worth, just her little sister, more than capable of being her big sister's rock when she needed it.

CHAPTER SIXTEEN

JOEL RAN A finger around the collar of his shirt and scanned the heaving room.

This was torture.

New York's finest all turned out as if they'd just stepped out of *The Great Gatsby*, him included, as Hart Hotel's speakeasy-style rum bar played host to his sister's engagement party.

The air was alive with laughter and chatter, the music from the pianist adding to the buzz, and all he wanted to do was turn around and head back out, but he was done running.

Forcing himself to the bar, he caught the bartender's eye. 'Double rum, neat.'

'Which one, sir?'

He leaned against the counter, rubbed a hand over his face. 'Any.'

Because any kind of rum would transport him back to Mustique, back to Jessie…he'd think his sister was purposefully adding to his torture if she hadn't booked it with Brendan long before he'd even met the woman who had dogged his every waking moment since. But of course Brendan would offer up the use of his hotel… He'd likely be hosting the wedding celebrations too somewhere across the globe, something Joel would already know if he'd paid more attention, been around more…

A squeal to his left had him wincing and he turned just in time to open his arms to a fast-approaching Simone, her smile and blue eyes bright, the feathers from her headband tickling his nose as she hugged him tight.

'You made it! I'm so happy you made it!' She pressed away from him, stared up into his eyes and…damned if he couldn't see tears in hers.

He forced a smile over the punch to the gut. 'I'm sorry you had to doubt it.'

She shook her head. 'Doesn't matter.' Though the wobble to her cherry-red bottom lip told him otherwise. 'I'm just so glad you're here now. Mum will be so pleased.'

He scanned the room, looking for the woman in question. He'd yet to see her since his arrival in the city. She'd been whisked away to Europe on some last-minute trip and had arrived back that morning.

'She's over there…' Simone turned and gestured in the direction of the piano, where the staircase beyond helped create a secluded corner. 'I warn you, though, she's like a giddy schoolgirl.'

'She's what?'

Simone simply smiled. 'You'll see…'

'Well, I'll be…' Simon approached, his blond hair slicked back, his suit matching his twin sister's, his smile less so. 'You made it, then.'

He deserved the reservation in his brother's tone, the look in his eye too, and he opened his mouth to deliver another apology when his back took a pounding.

'Hey, big brother, you're a sight for sore eyes!' Jonathan tugged him in for a bear hug that cut off his ability to breathe.

'Yeah, yeah, okay, it's good to see you too!' he choked out. 'I'd like to make it through the evening though, so if you can release my lungs...'

Jonathan chuckled. 'Sorry, buddy.'

Simone shook her head. 'He doesn't know his own strength since he's become something of a bear.'

'Will you quit with the bear, Sim? You make me sound hairy.'

'If the shoe fits,' she teased.

The anxious knot in his gut eased with their camaraderie. He was back where he belonged, but Simon's gaze remained more watchful than warm. 'Come on,' he said. 'I'll take you to see Mum—she's been waiting for you.'

'It's okay. I can take...' The subtle shake of his brother's head put paid to that idea and he muttered, 'I'm only half an hour late.'

'An eternity in her book,' Simone reminded him. 'And once you're done catching up, I'll see if I can extract my fiancé from his drinking buddies. We have something we want to ask you...'

He nodded, the guilt making a sharp return.

You're here now, though, that's what matters.
Simone had said it herself.

'Don't stress too much, brother,' Jonathan called after them. 'Nothing's gonna burst Mum's bubble, so I'd say you're pretty safe.'

Simon scoffed into his drink and Joel frowned. 'What's going on?'

'Mum has a boyfriend.'

'Mum has a *what*?'

Simon looked at him and that was when he realised—the wary look, the watchful eye, it wasn't about him, it was about this…the situation he was walking into. 'Look, I know you and Dad were close. Closer than any of us. But she's in love and she's happy, ridiculously so.'

He swallowed, the weird twisting sensation in his gut making him feel all kinds of nauseous. 'She's seeing someone else?'

'You make it sound like she's having an affair.'

'No. I just…' He raked a hand through his hair, sucked in a breath to ease the demons within. 'Why didn't anyone say anything?'

'Do you really need to ask that? It's hardly the sort of thing you tell someone over the phone, and we've been trying to get you to visit. Hell, Mum's been doing everything she could to get you back so that she could introduce you before today.'

'A warning would have been nice.'

'Too late now.'

The crowd seemed to part, his mother's table

coming into sight, and it stopped him in his tracks. She was glowing, radiant even. He'd blame it on the bronze sequins in her dress and matching head-piece if it weren't for the sparkle in her eyes, the softness to her smile... Love.

His mother was in *love*.

'He's a good man, Joel,' his brother said, quietly. 'And he loves her too. Just give him a chance, yeah? Heaven knows, she deserves it.'

His mother chose that moment to turn, her eyes lighting on them and widening in obvious disbelief.

'Joel!' She launched to her feet.

The man beside her rose too, not that Joel had taken him in yet. He was too busy taking in the news.

'You going to make her come over here after she's waited this long to see you again?' Simon murmured under his breath.

'All right, all right...'

He hurried towards her, leaving his brother behind and fixing his smile in place as his brain raced.

'Oh, Joel!' She reached up to cup his face in both hands. 'It's *so* good to see you.'

He kissed her cheek as she released him. 'You too, Mum.'

His eyes drifted to the dark-haired man standing beside her, grey at the temples, his brown eyes sharp as they assessed him back.

'Hi.' He held out his hand. 'I'm Joel.'

'I know who you are.' The man's smile softened his gaze, his handshake surprisingly firm. 'It's good to meet you at last—I've heard a lot about you.'

'I wish I could say the same.'

His mother's eyes flitted between them, an awkward flush to her cheeks. 'Joel, this is Arthur, my—my boyfriend.'

'Simon just told me…' He didn't mean to sound so disconnected, but never in a million years had he expected this. 'Care to fill me in?'

She gave an edgy laugh. 'Take a seat and we will…'

He pulled out a chair as they settled back into their previous position, Arthur taking his mother's hand and squeezing it, supporting her in the face of her absentee son, and Joel clenched his jaw.

'You've missed quite a bit, darling…'

He forced himself to relax into his seat, sip at his rum and listen to his mother tell him how they'd met, how it had felt as if it was meant to be, all the while Joel's eyes were fixed on his mother's hand in Arthur's, the wedding band that had switched fingers, the obvious intimacy and affection.

Arthur cleared his throat, eyed Joel's glass that was somehow empty in his hand. 'Looks like we could all do with another drink. Can I get you one, Joel?'

'Please,' he managed to say.

'Same again?'

He nodded, numbly. 'Rum. Any kind.'

Once he was out of earshot his mother leaned in, her hand soft upon Joel's on the tabletop.

'I'm sorry you're finding out like this, love. I would have told you, but it never felt right over the phone, and you were already so distant.'

'You still could have told me.'

'I was worried about how you'd take it. You and your father were always so close, and after Katie—'

'You're going to blame this on her?' he threw across the table, regretting it immediately as her eyes widened, the wound he'd inflicted unfair and vast. 'I'm sorry, I didn't…'

He broke off, losing his words, his ability to explain.

'It's okay. I was going to say that you know better than most what it feels like to lose the love of your life and that the idea of moving on seems so impossible. Of all my children, you were the one I was worried about telling the most.'

'It's a shock. I can't lie.'

She gave him a grave smile. 'I know. It was for me too. I didn't expect to meet someone else. I thought that was me done.'

Joel frowned. Done. It was a strange way to put it…but then, wasn't that how he felt? Done. Over with.

Wasn't that why he'd lived the last two years to the max, trying to feel alive again, trying to feel whole…and yet, only with Jessie had he felt that buzz in his veins and peace in his heart again.

'I felt guilty at first, so very guilty. But then I realised that loving Arthur didn't take anything away from my love for your father…it just gave me a second chance at happiness.'

'And he does that? Arthur? He makes you happy?'

'Very much so… I was lost when your father died, a mess, and the idea of spending the rest of my life alone… I know I have you kids but it's not the same as a life partner, someone to share the highs and the lows with.'

Her words teased at the Jessie-shaped wound that had yet to heal…the wound he wasn't sure *how* to heal.

'And in all honesty, I don't think your father would have wanted me to spend the rest of my life alone.'

He swallowed and she leaned in closer, brushed a stray lock behind his ear, a move he hadn't experienced her do since his teens.

'And Katie wouldn't want you to either, love. You must know that deep down?'

His eyes flared into hers. 'Why are you making this about me?'

She pressed her lips together.

'Has someone said something to you? Did Brendan…?'

Her cheeks coloured beneath her make-up. 'He said you'd met someone…'

He shook his head, physically recoiling as Jessie's smile, vibrant hair, compassionate eyes filled his vision…

'So, it's true?'

He couldn't speak, couldn't breathe.

'Oh, Joel. I know how you loved Katie, you will always love Katie, but that doesn't mean you can't find it again…'

He shook his head, trying to block her out, block Jessie out too. 'Don't, Mum.'

'But you need to hear this, love.' Her expression was so earnest, filled with her love for him, for his late father, for Arthur. 'Don't let guilt and grief take away the chance of finding happiness again. I almost did but look at me now. I'm happy, happier than I thought possible. And you have so many years left to live, do you really not want that for yourself?'

'I don't know what I want…' Only he did, and he'd let it go.

'Then try this—close your eyes and look to your future.'

'Mum…' He wanted to laugh at her but he had no humour left.

'I haven't seen you in too long, Joel, so please,

humour me. Close your eyes and imagine it. Do you see yourself alone?'

Slowly he did as she asked, closed his eyes and tried to visualise the future. Him. Alone. And there was nothing but darkness.

'Now think of it with her...'

He did. He thought of Jessie, and the future lit up like a well-adorned Christmas tree. Projecting hope and happiness and family. So many experiences still to share, so much joy and laughter... and then he thought of Katie in her hospital bed and the fuse to the fairy lights blew, his eyes flying open.

'I can't go through that pain again.'

She put her hand back on his. 'There's nothing to say you will, but, given the choice, would you have chosen *not* to have met Katie? Not to have had the years you did together?'

'I'd take away the ones where I was missing,' he was quick to say, his voice raw. 'I loved Dad. I did. But his work ethic, *my* work ethic, robbed me of that time. I don't blame him for showing me the way, I blame myself. For not being there, for not seeing...not noticing...'

'It wouldn't have changed things, love. She was ill. There was nothing you could do.'

'I could have been a better husband.'

'And I could have been a better wife. We all make mistakes, it's how we learn from them and—'

'And move on. Now you sound like someone else.'

She gave a small smile. 'Someone wise and all-knowing, I hope.'

The hint of a smile touched his lips. 'She'd like to think so.'

'It's true, Joel, what's happened in the past doesn't stop you from being a better husband in the future.'

Better husband...

Her words messed with his head, his heart. Was that fair? To learn from the mistakes he'd made with the love of his life and allow himself to love another better? It didn't feel right and yet...

'You need to forgive yourself, darling. Forgive yourself and give yourself the freedom to feel again. I had forty-five years with your father and I had to share it with his work just as Katie did with you. I don't hold it against him—he gave us all a good life, just as you did with Katie, and she felt the same. You know that deep down. You made her happy.'

'But...' He gritted his teeth against the pain and the tears that he refused to let fall tonight of all nights. 'It feels wrong.'

'I know. I felt that way in the beginning, like my love for Arthur betrayed your father, but it grew without my permission...' she gave a soft laugh '...love does that, you know.'

He thought of Jessie, of their fling that had grown to be so much more…

'One morning we were talking over breakfast in Venice and the next it was dinner and the next we were sightseeing across Europe… We've just been back for our one-year anniversary.'

He started. 'One *year*? You've been together a year and I'm only finding out now?'

She grimaced. 'It took me a while to tell anyone…falling in love is one thing, getting past the guilt is another. Simone found out first—she saw us together and, well, that girl can get blood out of a stone. She encouraged me to come clean with your brothers but no one wanted you to find out over the phone, least of all me.'

'I'm surprised the press haven't made a big deal of it.'

'Why would they? I'm old news now, my children are the future, and you all give the press enough ammo to leave me alone.'

Her eyes sparked with teasing disapproval and he huffed. 'They write what they want anyway.'

'I know. But I'm hoping there's something to the story Brendan told me. He seems to think this girl is in love with you.'

His heart warmed and contracted in one.

'I take it from your face he's right.'

'She told me she was.'

'And how do you feel about her?'

He couldn't answer without cracking.

'Listen, Joel, my life with Arthur is very different to what I had with your father, but it's no less fulfilling. I'm happy again, really, truly happy, and I want that for you.'

'I'm happy for you, Mum.'

'You mean that?'

He did. Seeing the light back in his mother's eyes, the sparkle…she looked ten years younger—how could he not be happy for her? 'Of course.'

'Then why can't you want it for yourself too? If there's a chance you could find love again with this girl, don't throw it away.'

'What if I already have? What if it's too late?'

'Walk away now and it will be. Go to her, tell her the truth. At the very least, you owe her those words in return.'

CHAPTER SEVENTEEN

JESSIE STARED AT the brochures laid out on the coffee table, her open laptop perched in the centre, and sighed. She was getting nowhere.

Her inheritance from Mum gave her options. It meant she could go back to university, study something new, extend her career break…but she was struggling to feel inspired.

She feared the ability to feel the fire in her veins, the excitement, the thrill of something new, had gone away with Joel and she wouldn't get it back.

That and the fact that every time she thought of moving on she inevitably *thought* of Joel and everything he'd done for her to get her to this point. The joy he'd brought her, the confidence, the fight to go after what she wanted…

And how had she repaid him?

By feeding his guilt over abandoning his family and his business, meddling in his life, and then backing him into a corner after only a few weeks of knowing him by declaring her love for him. Declaring her love when she'd known he was still in love with Katie.

It hadn't been fair, and heaven knew what damage she'd inflicted. Yes, she had a broken heart, but what about Joel…?

The only saving grace was that she knew he'd attended his sister's engagement party—she'd seen the pictures in the press to prove it. And he'd looked good. Too good. But she'd been starved of him for a month. He could look haggard and she'd still be mooning over him.

He'd been into the office too. Hannah had told her on one of the few occasions she'd dared ask after him.

All good signs, surely?

So why didn't that make her feel any better?

You know why…because he's moving on with his life just as he promised, and all without you.

She ignored the voice and reached for her phone, brought up his contact details, something she did numerous times a day, and fought the same battle—just one message. One message to see how he was, to reassure herself, to say sorry for overstepping and…and then what?

She threw her phone down with a groan and flopped back on the sofa. She'd done enough damage, said enough, confessed enough…

She should be moving on just as he so clearly was.

Molly, her mother's cat, rubbed up against her knee, its meow as pathetic as she felt. 'Yeah, yeah, I know, honey.' She scratched her head. 'We don't need a stinky man to make us happy but—'

The doorbell rang and Molly scarpered. She checked her watch. It was a bit late for cold-callers and the few friends she had in the village would usually message before coming round.

Scraping her hair back into a messy bun, she headed for the door…her oversized sweater decent enough if a little threadbare. Her bunny slippers perhaps a little less so.

She could see the outline of someone tall through the glass. Someone tall and broad and very definitely male.

'Have you sent me a stinky man?' she said to her mother's picture on the console table in the hall, unlatching the door and tugging it open a crack. She gasped, the ground seeming to fall away beneath her as she clung to the door to keep herself up.

'Joel?'

She staggered back a step, blinking rapidly. No, it couldn't be, but those eyes, that lopsided smile…

'Jessie.'

That voice.

She took a short breath, then another, her thudding heart threatening to break free of her ribcage. 'What are you…? Why are you here?'

Because there was only one reason she could think of and she didn't want to let that hope in… every doorbell ring, every phone call for the last few weeks she'd held on to that hope and had it dashed. And gradually it had eaten away at her. But now…now he was here.

'I needed to see you.'

Her heart skipped a beat and she tamped it down, clenched her fists. It doesn't mean he loves you. He's *told* you he can't love you.

He'd never denied the chemistry though.

'What we had is over, Joel. You made that clear. And I'm not up for any more "fun", so if you're here for a booty call you've had a wasted trip.'

She went to close the door before her heart intervened, but he stepped forward, pressed his palm against the frame.

'Please, Jessie, I came to talk, nothing more. There's something I need to tell you.'

'I think you've already told me enough.'

'No—No, I haven't. I owe you the truth.'

'You were pretty blunt with the—'

'Jessie…?' Stella from next door paused on her nightly dog walk, her concerned frown as she took in Joel's presence enough to have Jessie smiling wide. 'Is everything okay, dear?'

'Everything's fine, Stella. My friend here is just visiting.'

Stella nodded but her sharpened gaze was unconvinced. They were going to be the subject of the village's gossip mill come morning.

'You'd best come inside before we gain an audience,' Jessie told Joel under her breath as she waved Stella on and stepped aside to let him in.

He crossed over the threshold, his 'Thank you' gruff with relief.

Molly came up to him, purring around his legs as Jessie swung the door closed.

'Traitor,' she murmured to the furry miscreant. 'Not allergic, are you?'

'No.'

'Pity.'

His lips quirked, a spark of humour in his eyes that she refused to react to. Nothing about this was funny.

He broke your heart, she reminded herself as she strode for the kitchen without waiting for him, *and you broke him*.

Guilt stabbed at her, weakening her resolve. But apologising over the phone hadn't felt right. Apologising face to face while resisting the pull between them felt nigh on impossible, her heart too weak not to cross the line she told him she wasn't willing to cross. Not again.

She pulled the wine she'd opened earlier from the fridge and flicked him a look. 'Want one?'

'Please.'

He held back in the doorway as she poured two glasses, her defiant gaze refusing to stay off him. He wore jeans and a navy T-shirt, both far too snug for her sanity. His hair was its usual mop of blonde, his eyes blisteringly blue, his mouth too full and alluring. She'd kissed that mouth a hundred times over, fantasised about it a hundred times more, and still she wanted him.

Why couldn't her body get with the programme

and realise he wasn't hers to want, to crave, to love…?

He'd made that painfully clear.

'Here.' She shoved a glass at him, debated going back into the living room with all her brochures everywhere and decided against it. She didn't want him to witness the state of her life, her confusion, her mess…a mess that wouldn't be so messy if it weren't for him and the mark he'd unintentionally left on her heart.

'Thank you.' He took it but his eyes never left hers, their depths desperately seeking something in her own…or at least that was the impression they gave.

She huffed away the nonsensical thought and stepped away before his proximity had her doing something stupid. Like begging his forgiveness, or worse, taking back her refusal to enjoy more 'fun'.

Putting the ancient wooden table that had seen many a family dinner over the years between them, she leant back against the counter, folded her arms.

'Well…talk.'

His throat bobbed, the tanned length as distracting as the rest of him. It wasn't fair. How could he look so good when she looked as if she'd got dressed in the dark using a dumpster for a wardrobe.

'You look incredible.'

She choked on her wine. 'I thought you were here to speak the truth.'

'I am…' He stepped towards her and she backed away, shook her head.

'Oh, no, you stay right there.'

He stalled, his jaw pulsing, his brows drawing together.

'Please, Joel, just say what you've come to say so I can get on with my evening.'

'You have plans?'

'Yes.' She didn't, other than a date with the TV, but he didn't need to know that.

He hesitated, then, 'I've missed you.' It came out raw, honest, but of course he'd missed her— there was no denying the sex had been out of this world—and she scoffed. 'I'm serious, Jessie, I've missed you more than I ever thought it was possible to miss someone.'

'Now I know you're lying. You lost your wife, Joel, the love of your life. You know exactly what it's like.' It was brutal, frank, cruel even, but she had to do this. She needed to be as blunt as he'd been because there could be no beating around the bush with this. Her heart was too exposed, too vulnerable.

'That was different,' he said quietly, placing his untouched wine on the side. 'She was gone and there was no getting her back. With you…you were very much alive, and I'd pushed you away.'

She opened her mouth to refute it, to tell him that she'd been the one doing the pushing, but the guilt of it held her tongue.

'Knowing you were here, living your life while I chose to stay away, was torture, and I don't want to choose that path any more.'

She gave a delirious laugh, threw back her wine as she stared at him in disbelief, hating the way the setting sun came through the window and shrouded him in warm, inviting amber, enhancing his tan, his eyes, the cut to his jaw…his words that were teasing at her heart, reigniting the hope…

'What are you saying, Joel? Because you made it perfectly clear that there's no future for us, that you've loved and lost and never intend to go there again. And I may be strong and independent, but I still have feelings and I'm not willing to risk my heart again for a friend-with-benefits arrangement…no matter how good our chemistry is.'

'I'm not asking you to be my friend.'

She choked on more wine, her cheeks flushing. 'If you're suggesting some weird arrangement where—'

'I'm telling you I want to date you.'

Her laugh was off-the-charts incredulous now. 'You want to *date* me?'

He nodded, unperturbed. 'I want to go back to the beginning and do this properly. I want to make you fall in love with me all over again because I promise to get it right this time.'

She was shaking her head, her heart an erratic beat in her ears. Was he *serious*? 'I don't understand.'

'Then let me make it perfectly clear, in words that you can't misconstrue…' He stepped towards her and this time she was too stunned to object, too stunned to move. She couldn't feel her legs any more…her mouth wouldn't even close. He took the glass from her unresisting fingers, placed it on the side, reached up to cup her face, which warmed and tingled beneath his touch, as traitorous as the cat had been.

'Jessie…' he searched her gaze, his thumbs a light caress across her cheekbones '…I am in love with you.'

Her breath left her, her eyes stung and she blinked, blinked again, but her vision wouldn't clear. She couldn't be hearing him right, she couldn't…

'I am so head over heels, crazy in love with you that the last month without you has driven me insane. I know I've given you no reason to trust me. I know I need to earn that back. I know you probably hate me for what I did, and I can't blame you, but *please,* give me a chance to prove myself to you.'

'But—how—how can you love me,' tears strained at her words, 'after everything I did?'

'What do you mean?'

'Joel, you gave me so much and I treated you so badly. I turned the tables on you. I broke our agreement to a short-term fling. I backed you into a corner by confessing my feelings after only a few weeks. I pushed you so hard when you were still grieving for Katie, when I *knew* you were still grieving. I tried to push my life philosophy, my mother's philosophy, onto you…' She was rambling, her head shaking in his hold, her guilt flowing from her lips, tears rolling down her cheeks. 'I made you feel all that guilt for leaving your family, your business, I meddled when I had no right to. I'm sorry. I'm so sorry…'

'Hush, baby, hush. You were right to do all those things.'

'But I—I don't understand. Why are you saying this now? What's changed?'

She needed to understand, she was *desperate* to understand, to believe…

He gave the smallest of smiles. 'There's something of a story to it—one that started with you and ended with my mother.'

She frowned, hiccupped on a sob. 'Your mother?'

'She's found love again. Forty-five years she had with my father and now she has someone else.'

Her frown deepened. 'So your mother has a new man and *that* makes it okay for you to be with me?'

'I know how it sounds, but I can explain…it really wasn't easy, seeing her with another man, wondering how my father would feel, analysing how I felt about it, but I realised that none of it mattered in the face of her joy, her happiness. She's found a new lease of life, and how can I judge something or someone for giving her that?'

She looked into his eyes, saw the truth in what he was saying and what it meant for her, for them. 'And I'm that for you?'

The smile returned, the sparkle in his gaze. 'Yes. You're my Arthur.'

'Your *Arthur*?'

'My mother's second chance.'

She gave a choked laugh, still struggling to believe this was real. That he was here confessing his love, wanting a future.

'It was weird seeing them together, but it was also amazing, and to realise I could have it too, that it was okay to want it…'

'Did you talk to her about us?'

'She already knew. Brendan told her.'

She smiled softly. 'Telling tales…'

'He's been doing it all my life—why would he change now?'

'You love him really.'

'I do… Just as I love you.'

She gulped back the rising tears. 'Not in the same way I hope.'

He chuckled. 'No…' But then his gaze turned sombre, his mouth a grim line. 'I'm not here to mess you around, Jessie. Hell, I had to prove my intentions to Hannah and Brendan before they'd hand over your address, and if I can convince them I hope I can convince you too. I'm not going to lie either, I'm still broken. I'll want to wrap you in cotton wool, cart you to the doctor any time you're feeling peaky, I'll be a royal pain in your arse—'

'You mean you won't be forcing me to jump off cliffs or surf in shark-infested waters or race buggies with vertical drops either side…'

He chuckled. 'Absolutely not.'

'You're going to be boring?' She pouted up at him.

'I never said boring…just a toned-down version of myself.'

She cocked her head to the side. 'So, jumping off rocks not cliffs, surfing without sharks, racing without drops…'

He nodded. 'And while we're doing all that, I'll do everything in my power to prove my love for you.'

His blue eyes blazed with his sincerity, with his love.

'You really love me?'

'I really do, though saying it doesn't feel enough any more.'

She choked back her tears, reached her hands into his hair. 'In that case, just shut up and kiss me.'

He huffed out a laugh. 'Does that mean you forgive me?'

'If you can forgive me…'

'There's nothing to forgive. I mean it. I love you so much.'

'I love you too.'

And then she kissed him so deeply, so thoroughly, there could be no doubt in his mind that she meant it.

For the first time in for ever, the cottage felt like home again because he was in it.

Her love. Her life. Her future.

No regrets, Mum.

* * * * *

*Look out for the next story in the
Billionaires for the Rose Sisters duet
Coming soon!*

*And if you enjoyed this story
check out these other great reads from
Rachael Stewart*

**My Year with the Billionaire
The Billionaire Behind the Headlines
Secrets Behind the Billionaire's Return**

All available now!